IN LUCK AT LAST

WALTER BESANT

In Luck at Last

Walter Besant

© 1st World Library, 2006
PO Box 2211
Fairfield, IA 52556
www.1stworldlibrary.com
First Edition

LCCN: 2006936249

Softcover ISBN: 978-1-4218-3113-8
Hardcover ISBN: 978-1-4218-3013-1
eBook ISBN: 978-1-4218-3213-5

Purchase *"In Luck at Last"*
as a traditional bound book at:
www.1stWorldLibrary.com/purchase.asp?ISBN=978-1-4218-3113-8

1st World Library is a literary, educational organization
dedicated to:

- Creating a free internet library of downloadable ebooks

- Hosting writing competitions and offering book
  publishing scholarships.

Interested in more 1st World Library books?
contact: literacy@1stworldlibrary.com
Check us out at: www.1stworldlibrary.com

1st World Library Literary Society

Giving Back to the World

"If you want to work on the core problem, it's early school literacy."
                    - James Barksdale, former CEO of Netscape

"No skill is more crucial to the future of a child, or to a democratic and prosperous society, than literacy."

                                   - Los Angeles Times

Literacy... means far more than learning how to read and write... The aim is to transmit... knowledge and promote social participation."
                                        - UNESCO

"Literacy is not a luxury, it is a right and a responsibility. If our world is to meet the challenges of the twenty-first century we must harness the energy and creativity of all our citizens."

                              - President Bill Clinton

"Parents should be encouraged to read to their children, and teachers should be equipped with all available techniques for teaching literacy, so the varying needs and capacities of individual kids can be taken into account."
                                     - Hugh Mackay

CHAPTER I

WITHIN THREE WEEKS

If everyone were allowed beforehand to choose and select for himself the most pleasant method of performing this earthly pilgrimage, there would be, I have always thought, an immediate run upon that way of getting to the Delectable Mountains which is known as the Craft and Mystery of Second-hand Bookselling. If, further, one were allowed to select and arrange the minor details—such, for instance, as the "pitch" and the character of the shop, it would seem desirable that, as regards the latter, the kind of bookselling should be neither too lofty nor too mean—that is to say, that one's ambition would not aspire to a great collector's establishment, such as one or two we might name in Piccadilly, the Haymarket, or New Bond Street; these should be left to those who greatly dare and are prepared to play the games of Speculation and of Patience; nor, on the other hand, would one choose an open cart at the beginning of the Whitechapel Road, or one of the shops in Seven Dials, whose stock-in-trade consists wholly of three or four boxes outside the door filled with odd volumes at twopence apiece. As for "pitch" or situation, one would wish it to be somewhat retired, but not too much; one would not, for instance, willingly be thrown away in Hoxton, nor would one languish in the obscurity of Kentish Town; a second-hand bookseller must not be so far removed from the haunts of men as to place him practically beyond the reach of the collector; nor, on the other hand, should he be planted in a busy thoroughfare—the noise of many vehicles, the hurry of quick footsteps, the swift current of anxious humanity are out of harmony with the atmosphere of a second-hand bookshop. Some suggestion of external repose is absolutely necessary; there must be some stillness in the air; yet the thing itself belongs essentially to the city—no one can imagine a second-hand bookshop beside green fields— so that there should be some murmur and perceptible hum of mankind always present in the ear. Thus there are half-a-dozen bookshops in King William Street, Strand, which seem to enjoy every possible advantage of position, for they are in the very heart of London, but yet are not exposed to the full noise and tumult of that overflowing tide which surges round Charing Cross. Again, there are streets north of Holborn and Oxford Street most pleasantly situated for the second-hand bookseller, and there are streets where he ought not to be, where he has no business, and where his presence jars. Could we, for instance, endure to see the shop of a second-hand bookseller established in Cheapside?

Perhaps, however, the most delightful spot in all London for a second-hand bookshop is that occupied by Emblem's in the King's Road, Chelsea.

It stands at the lower end of the road, where one begins to realize and thoroughly feel the influences of that ancient and lordly suburb. At this end of the road there are rows of houses with old-fashioned balconies; right and left of it there are streets which in the summer and early autumn are green, yellow, red, and golden with their masses of creepers; squares which look as if, with the people living in them, they must belong to the year eighteen hundred; neither a day before nor a day after; they lie open to the road, with their gardens full of trees. Cheyne Walk and the old church, with its red-brick tower, and the new Embankment, are all so close that they seem part and parcel of the King's Road. The great Hospital is within five minutes' walk, and sometimes the honest veterans themselves may be seen wandering in the road. The air is heavy with associations and memories. You can actually smell the fragrance of the new-made Chelsea buns, fresh from the oven,

Walter Besant

just as you would a hundred years ago. You may sit with dainty damsels, all hoops and furbelows, eating custards at the Bun-house; you may wander among the rare plants of the Botanic Gardens. The old great houses rise, shadowy and magnificent, above the modern terraces; Don Saltero's Coffee-House yet opens its hospitable doors; Sir Thomas More meditates again on Cheyne Walk; at dead of night the ghosts of ancient minuet tunes may be heard from the Rotunda of Ranelagh Gardens, though the new barracks stand upon its site; and along the modern streets you may fancy that if you saw the ladies with their hoop petticoats, and the gentlemen with their wigs and their three-cornered hats and swords, you would not be in the least astonished.

Emblem's is one of two or three shops which stand together, but it differs from its neighbors in many important particulars. For it has no plate-glass, as the others have; nor does it stand like them with open doors; nor does it flare away gas at night; nor is it bright with gilding and fresh paint; nor does it seek to attract notice by posters and bills. On the contrary, it retains the old, small, and unpretending panes of glass which it has always had; in the evening it is dimly lighted, and it closes early; its door is always shut, and although the name over the shop is dingy, one feels that a coat of paint, while it would certainly freshen up the place, would take something from its character. For a second-hand bookseller who respects himself must present an exterior which has something of faded splendor, of worn paint and shabbiness. Within the shop, books line the walls and cumber the floor. There are an outer and an inner shop; in the former a small table stands among the books, at which Mr. James, the assistant, is always at work cataloguing, when he is not tying up parcels; sometimes even with gum and paste repairing the slighter ravages of time— foxed bindings and close-cut margins no man can repair. In the latter, which is Mr. Emblem's sanctum, there are chairs and a table, also covered with books, a writing-desk, a small safe, and a glass case, wherein are secured the more costly books in stock. Emblem's, as must be confessed, is no longer quite what it was in former days; twenty, thirty, or forty years ago that glass case was filled with precious treasures. In those days, if a man wanted a book of county history, or of genealogy, or of heraldry, he knew where was his best chance of finding it, for Emblem's, in its prime and heyday, had its specialty. Other books treating on more frivolous subjects, such as science, belles lettres, art, or politics, he would consider, buy, and sell again; but he took little pride in them. Collectors of county histories, however, and genealogy-hunters and their kind, knew that at Emblem's, where they would be most likely to get what they wanted, they would have to pay the market price for it.

There is no patience like the patience of a book-collector; there is no such industry given to any work comparable with the thoughtful and anxious industry with which he peruses the latest catalogues; there is no care like unto that which rends his mind before the day of auction or while he is still trying to pick up a bargain; there are no eyes so sharp as those which pry into the contents of a box full of old books, tumbled together, at sixpence apiece. The bookseller himself partakes of the noble enthusiasm of the collector, though he sells his collection; like the amateur, the professional moves heaven and earth to get a bargain: like him, he rejoices as much over a book which has been picked up below its price, as over a lost sheep which has returned into the fold. But Emblem is now old, and Emblem's shop is no longer what it was to the collector of the last generation.

It was an afternoon in late September, and in this very year of grace, eighteen hundred and eighty-four. The day was as sunny and warm as any of the days of its predecessor Augustus the Gorgeous, but yet there was an autumnal feeling in the air which made itself felt even in streets where there were no red and yellow Virginia creepers, no square gardens with long trails of mignonette and banks of flowering nasturtiums. In fact, you cannot anywhere escape the autumnal feeling, which begins about the middle of September. It makes old people think with sadness that the grasshopper is a burden in the land, and that the almond-tree is about to flourish; but the young it fills with a vinous and intoxicated rejoicing, as if the time of feasting, fruits, harvests, and young wine, strong and fruity, was upon the world. It made Mr. James—his surname has never been ascertained, but man and boy, Mr. James has been at Emblem's for twenty-five years and more—leave his table where he was preparing the forthcoming catalogue, and go to the open door, where he wasted a good minute and a half in gazing up at the clear sky and down the sunny street. Then he stretched his arms and returned to his work, impelled by the sense of duty rather than by the scourge of necessity, because there was no hurry about the catalogue and most of the books in it were rubbish, and at that season of the year few customers could be expected, and there were no parcels to tie up and send out. He went back to his work, therefore, but he left the door partly open in order to enjoy the sight of the warm sunshine. Now for Emblem's to have its door open, was much as if Mr. Emblem himself should so far forget his self-respect as to sit in his shirt-sleeves. The shop had been rather dark, the window being full of books, but now through the open door there poured a little stream of sunshine, reflected from some far off window. It fell upon a row of old eighteenth century volumes, bound in dark and rusty leather, and did so light up and glorify the dingy bindings and faded gold, that they seemed fresh from the binder's hands, and just ready for the noble purchaser, long since dead and gone, whose book plate they bore. Some of this golden stream fell also upon the head of the assistant—it was a red head, with fiery red eyes, red eyebrows, bristly and thick, and sharp thin features to match—and it gave him the look of one who is dragged unwillingly into the sunlight. However, Mr. James took no notice of the sunshine, and went on with his cataloguing almost as if he liked that kind of work. There are many people who seem to like dull work, and they would not be a bit more unhappy if they were made to take the place of Sisyphus, or transformed into the damsels who are condemned to toil continually at the weary work of pouring water into a sieve. Perhaps Sisyphus does not so much mind the continual going up and down hill. "After all," he might say, "this is better than the lot of poor Ixion. At all events, I have got my limbs free." Ixion, on the other hand, no doubt, is full of pity for his poor friend Sisyphus. "I, at least," he says, "have no work to do. And the rapid motion of the wheel is in sultry weather sometimes pleasant."

Behind the shop, where had been originally the "back parlor," in the days when every genteel house in Chelsea had both its front and back parlor—the latter for sitting and living in, the former for the reception of company—sat this afternoon the proprietor, the man whose name had stood above the shop for fifty years, the original and only Emblem. He was—nay, he is—for you may still find him in his place, and may make his acquaintance over a county history any day in the King's Road—he is an old man now, advanced in the seventies, who was born before the battle of Waterloo was fought, and can remember Chelsea when it was full of veterans wounded in battles fought long before the Corsican Attila was let loose upon the world. His face wears the peaceful and wise expression which belongs peculiarly to his profession. Other callings make a man look peaceful, but not all other callings make him look wise. Mr. Emblem was born by nature of a calm temperament,—otherwise he would not have been happy in his business; a smile lies generally upon his lips, and his eyes are soft and benign; his hair is white, and his face, once ruddy, is pale, yet not shrunk and seamed with furrows as happens to so many old men, but round and firm; like his chin and lips it is clean shaven; he wears a black coat extraordinarily shiny in the sleeve, and a black silk stock just as he used to wear in the thirties when he was young, and something of a dandy, and would show himself on a Saturday evening in the pit of Drury Lane; and the stock is fastened behind with a silver buckle. He is, in fact, a delightful old gentleman to look at and pleasant to converse with, and on his brow every one who can read may see, visibly stamped, the seal of a harmless and honest life. At the contemplation of such a man, one's opinion of humanity is sensibly raised, and even house-agents, plumbers, and suburban builders, feel that, after all, virtue may bring with, it some reward.

The quiet and warmth of the afternoon, unbroken to his

accustomed ear, as it would be to a stranger, by the murmurous roll of London, made him sleepy. In his hand he held a letter which he had been reading for the hundredth time, and of which he knew by heart every word; and as his eyes closed he went back in imagination to a passage in the past which it recalled.

He stood, in imagination, upon the deck of a sailing-ship—an emigrant ship. The year was eighteen hundred and sixty-four, a year when very few were tempted to try their fortunes in a country torn by civil war. With him were his daughter and his son-in-law, and they were come to bid the latter farewell.

"My dear—my dear," cried the wife, in her husband's arms, "come what may, I will join you in a year."

Her husband shook his head sadly.

"They do not want me here," he said; "the work goes into stronger and rougher hands. Perhaps over there we may get on better, and besides, it seems an opening."

If the kind of work which he wanted was given to stronger and rougher hands than his in England, far more would it be the case in young and rough America. It was journalistic work— writing work—that he wanted; and he was a gentleman, a scholar, and a creature of retired and refined tastes and manners. There are, perhaps, some still living who have survived the tempestuous life of the ordinary Fleet Street "newspaper man" of twenty or thirty years ago; perhaps one or two among these remember Claude Aglen—but he was so short a time with them that it is not likely; those who do remember him will understand that the way to success, rough and thorny for all, for such as Aglen was impossible.

"But you will think every day of little Iris?" said his wife. "Oh, my dear, if I were only going with you! And but for me you would be at home with your father, well and happy."

Then in his dream, which was also a memory, the old man saw how the young husband kissed and comforted his wife.

"My dear," said Claude, "if it were not for you, what happiness could I have in the world? Courage, my wife, courage and hope. I shall think of you and Iris all day and all night until we meet again."

And so they parted and the ship sailed away.

The old man opened his eyes and looked about him. It was a dream.

"It was twenty years ago," he said, "and Iris was a baby in arms. Twenty years ago, and he never saw his wife again. Never again! Because she died," he added after a pause; "my Alice died."

He shed no tears, being so old that the time of tears was well-nigh past—at seventy-five the eyes are drier than at forty, and one is no longer surprised or disappointed, and seldom even angry, whatever happens.

But he opened the letter in his hand and read it again mechanically. It was written on thin foreign paper, and the creases of the folds had become gaping rents. It was dated September, 1866, just eighteen years back.

"When you read these lines," the letter said, "I shall be in the silent land, whither Alice, my wife, has gone before me. It would be a strange thing only to think upon this journey which lies before me, and which I must take alone, had I time left for thinking. But I have not. I may last a week, or I may die in a few hours. Therefore, to the point.

"In one small thing we deceived you, Alice and I—my name is not Aglen at all; we took that name for certain reasons. Perhaps we were wrong, but we thought that as we were quite poor, and likely to remain poor, it would be well to keep our secret to ourselves. Forgive us both this suppression of the truth. We were made poor by our own voluntary act and deed, and because I married the only woman I loved.

"I was engaged to a girl whom I did not love. We had been brought up like brother and sister together, but I did not love her, though I was engaged to her. In breaking this engagement I angered my father. In marrying Alice I angered him still more.

"I now know that he has forgiven me; he forgave me on his death-bed; he revoked his former will and made me his sole heir—just as if nothing had happened to destroy his old affection—subject to one condition—viz., that the girl to whom I was first engaged should receive the whole income until I, or my heirs, should return to England in order to claim the inheritance.

"It is strange. I die in a wooden shanty, in a little Western town, the editor of a miserable little country paper. I have not money enough even to bury me, and yet, if I were at home, I might be called a rich man, as men go. My little Iris will be an heiress. At the very moment when I learn that I am my father's heir, I am struck down by fever; and now I know that I shall never get up again.

"It is strange. Yet my father sent me his forgiveness, and my wife is dead, and the wealth that has come is useless to me. Wherefore, nothing now matters much to me, and I know that you will hold my last wishes sacred.

"I desire that Iris shall be educated as well and thoroughly as you can afford; keep her free from rough and rude companions; make her understand that her father was a gentleman of ancient family; this knowledge will, perhaps, help to give her self-respect. If any misfortune should fall upon you, such as the loss of health or wealth, give the papers inclosed to a trustworthy solicitor, and bid him act as is best in the interests of Iris. If, as I hope, all will go well with you, do not open the papers until my child's twenty-first birthday; do not let her know until then that she is going to be rich; on her twenty-first birthday, open the papers and bid her claim her own.

"To the woman I wronged—I know not whether she has married or not—bid Iris carry my last message of sorrow at what has happened. I do not regret, and I have never regretted, that I married Alice. But, I gave her pain, for which I have never ceased to grieve. I have been punished for this breach of faith. You will find among the papers an account of all the circumstances connected with this engagement. There is also in the packet my portrait, taken when I was a lad of sixteen; give her that as well; there is the certificate of my marriage, my register of baptism, that of Iris's baptism, my signet ring—" "His arms"—the old man interrupted his reading—"his arms were: quarterly: first and fourth, two roses and a boar's head, erect; second and third, gules and fesse between—between—but I cannot remember what it was between—" He went on reading: "My father's last letter to me; Alice's letters, and one or two from yourself. If Iris should unhappily die before her twenty-first birthday, open these papers, find out from them the owner's name and address, seek her out, and tell her that she will never now be disturbed by any claimants to the estate."

The letter ended here abruptly, as if the writer had designed to add more, but was prevented by death.

For there was a postscript, in another hand, which stated: "Mr. Aglen died November 25th, 1866, and is buried in the cemetery of Johnson City, Ill."

The old man folded the letter carefully, and laid it on the table. Then he rose and walked across the room to the safe, which stood with open door in the corner furthest from the fireplace. Among its contents was a packet sealed and tied up in red tape, endorsed: "For Iris. To be given to her on her twenty-first birthday. From her father."

"It will be her twenty-first birthday," he said, "in three weeks. Then I must give her the packet. So—so—with the portrait of her father, and his marriage-certificate." He fell into a fit of musing, with the papers in his hand. "She will be safe, whatever happens to me; and as for me, if I lose her—of course I shall lose her. Why, what will it matter? Have I not lost all, except Iris? One must not be selfish. Oh, Iris, what a surprise—what a surprise I have in store for you!"

He placed the letter he had been reading within the tape which fastened the bundle, so that it should form a part of the communication to be made on Iris's birthday.

"There," he said, "now I shall read this letter no more. I wonder how many times I have read it in the last eighteen years, and how often I have wondered what the child's fortune would be? In three weeks—in three short weeks. Oh, Iris, if you only knew!"

He put back the letters and the packet, locked the safe, and resumed his seat.

The red-eyed assistant, still gumming and pasting his slips with punctilious regard to duty, had been following his master's movements with curiosity.

"Counting his investments again as usual," Mr. James murmured. "Ah! and adding 'em up! Always at it. Oh, what a trade it must have been once!"

Just then there appeared in the door a gentleman. He was quite shabby, and even ragged in his dress, but he was clearly a gentleman. He was no longer young; his shoulders were bent, and he had the unmistakable stamp and carriage of a student.

"Guv'nor's at home," said the assistant briefly.

The visitor walked into the sanctum. He had under his arm half-a-dozen volumes, which, without a word, he laid before

Mr. Emblem, and untied the string.

"You ought to know this book," he said without further introduction.

Mr. Emblem looked doubtfully at the visitor.

"You sold it to me twenty-five years ago," he went on, "for five pounds."

"I did. And I remember now. You are Mr. Frank Farrar. Why, it is twenty-five years ago!"

"I have bought no more books for twenty years and more," he replied.

"Sad—sad! Dear me—tut, tut!—bought no books? And you, Mr. Farrar, once my best customer. And now—you do not mean to say that you are going to sell—that you actually want to sell—this precious book?"

"I am selling, one by one, all my books," replied the other with a sigh. "I am going down hill, Emblem, fast."

"Oh, dear, dear!" replied the bookseller. "This is very sad. One cannot bear to think of the libraries being dispersed and sold off. And now yours, Mr. Farrar? Really, yours? Must it be?"

"Needs must," Mr. Farrar said with a sickly smile, "needs must when the devil drives. I have parted with half my books already. But I thought you might like to have this set, because they were once your own."

"So I should"—Mr. Emblem laid a loving hand upon the volumes—"so I should, Mr. Farrar, but not from you; not from you, sir. Why, you were almost my best customer—I think almost my very best—thirty years ago, when my trade was better than it is now. Yes, you gave me five pounds—or was it five pounds ten?—for this very work. And it is worth

Walter Besant

twelve pounds now—I assure you it is worth twelve pounds, if it is worth a penny."

"Will you give me ten pounds for it, then?" cried the other eagerly; "I want the money badly."

"No, I can't; but I will send you to a man who can and will. I do not speculate now; I never go to auctions. I am old, you see. Besides, I am poor. I will not buy your book, but I will send you to a man who will give you ten pounds for it, I am sure, and then he will sell it for fifteen." He wrote the address on a slip of paper. "Why, Mr. Farrar, if an old friend, so to speak, can put the question, why in the world—"

"The most natural thing," replied Mr. Farrar with a cold laugh; "I am old, as I told you, and the younger men get all the work. That is all. Nobody wants a genealogist and antiquary."

"Dear me, dear me! Why, Mr. Farrar, I remember now; you used to know my poor son-in-law, who is dead eighteen years since. I was just reading the last letter he ever wrote to me, just before he died. You used to come here and sit with him in the evening. I remember now. So you did."

"Thank you for your good will," said Mr. Farrar. "Yes, I remember your son-in-law. I knew him before his marriage."

"Did you? Before his marriage? Then—" He was going to add, "Then you can tell me his real name," but he paused, because it is a pity ever to acknowledge ignorance, and especially ignorance in such elementary matters as your son-in-law's name.

So Mr. Emblem checked himself.

"He ought to have been a rich man," Mr. Farrar continued; "but he quarreled with his father, who cut him off with a shilling, I suppose."

Then the poor scholar, who could find no market for his learned papers, tied up his books again and went away with hanging head.

"Ugh!" Mr. James, who had been listening, groaned as Mr. Farrar passed through the door. "Ugh! Call that a way of doing business? Why, if it had been me, I'd have bought the book off of that old chap for a couple o' pounds, I would. Ay, or a sov, so seedy he is, and wants money so bad. And I know who'd have given twelve pound for it, in the trade too. Call that carrying on business? He may well add up his investments every day, it he can afford to chuck such chances. Ah, but he'll retire soon." His fiery eyes brightened, and his face glowed with the joy of anticipation. "He must retire before long."

There came another visitor. This time it was a lanky boy, with, a blue bag over his shoulder and a notebook and pencil-stump in his hand. He nodded to the assistant as to an old friend with whom one may be at ease, set down his bag, opened his notebook, and nibbled his stump. Then he read aloud, with a comma or semicolon between each, a dozen or twenty titles. They were the names of the books which his employer wished to pick up. The red-eyed assistant listened, and shook his head. Then the boy, without another word, shouldered his bag and departed, on his way to the next second-hand book-shop.

He was followed, at a decent interval, by another caller. This time it was an old gentleman who opened the door, put in his head, and looked about him with a quick and suspicious glance. At sight of the assistant he nodded and smiled in the most friendly way possible, and came in.

"Good-morning, Mr. James; good-morning, my friend. Splendid weather. Pray don't disturb yourself. I am just having a look round—only a look round, you know. Don't move, Mr. James."

He addressed Mr. James, but he was looking at the shelves as he spoke, and, with the habit of a book-hunter, taking down the volumes, looking at the title-pages and replacing them; under his arm he carried a single volume in old leather binding.

Mr. James nodded his head, but did disturb himself; in fact, he rose with a scowl upon his face, and followed this polite old gentlemen all round the shop, placing himself close to his elbow. One might almost suppose that he suspected him, so close and assiduous was his assistance. But the visitor, accepting these attentions as if they were customary, and the result of high breeding, went slowly round the shelves, taking down book after book, but buying none. Presently he smiled again, and said that he must be moving on, and very politely thanked Mr. James for his kindness.

"Nowhere," he was so good as to say, "does one get so much personal kindness and attention as at Emblem's. Good-morning, Mr. James; good-morning, my friend."

Mr. James grunted; and closed the door after him.

"Ugh!" he said with disgust, "I know you; I know your likes. Want to make your set complete—eh? Want to sneak one of our books to do it with, don't you? Ah!" He looked into the back shop before he returned to his paste and his slips. "That was Mr. Potts, the great Queen Anne collector, sir. Most notorious book-snatcher in all London, and the most barefaced. Wanted our fourth volume of the 'Athenian Oracle.' I saw his eyes reached out this way, and that way, and always resting on that volume. I saw him edging along to the shelf. Got another odd volume just like it in his wicked old hand, ready to change it when I wasn't looking."

"Ah," said Mr. Emblem, waking up from his dream of Iris and her father's letter; "ah, they will try it on. Keep your eyes open, James."

"No thanks, as usual," grumbled Mr. James as he returned to his gum and his scissors. "Might as well have left him to snatch the book."

Here, however, James was wrong, because it is the first duty of an assistant to hinder and obstruct the book-snatcher, who carries on his work by methods of crafty and fraudulent exchange rather than by plain theft, which is a mere brutal way. For, first, the book-snatcher marks his prey; he finds the shop which has a set containing the volume which is missing in his own set; next, he arms himself with a volume which closely resembles the one he covets, and then, on pretense of turning over the leaves, he watches his opportunity to effect an exchange, and goes away rejoicing, his set complete. No collector, as is very well known, whether of books, coins, pictures, medals, fans, scarabs, book-plates, autographs, stamps, or anything else, has any conscience at all. Anybody can cut out slips and make a catalogue, but it requires a sharp assistant, with eyes all over his head like a spider, to be always on guard against this felonious and unscrupulous collector.

Next, there came two schoolboys together, who asked for and bought a crib to "Virgil;" and then a girl who wanted some cheap French reading-book. Just as the clock began to strike five, Mr. Emblem lifted his head and looked up. The shop-door opened, and there stepped in, rubbing his shoes on the mat as if he belonged to the house, an elderly gentleman of somewhat singular appearance. He wore a fez cap, but was otherwise dressed as an Englishman—in black frock coat, that is, buttoned up—except that his feet were incased in black cloth shoes, so that he went noiselessly. His hair was short and white, and he wore a small white beard; his skin was a rather dark brown; he was, in fact, a Hindoo, and his name was Lala Roy.

He nodded gravely to Mr. James and walked into the back shop.

"It goes well," he asked, "with the buying and the selling?"

"Surely, Lala, surely."

"A quiet way of buying and selling; a way fit for one who meditates," said the Hindoo, looking round. "Tell me, my friend, what ails the child? Is she sick?"

"The child is well, Lala."

"Her mind wandered this morning. She failed to perceive a simple method which I tried to teach her. I feared she might be ill."

"She is not ill, my friend, but I think her mind is troubled."

"She is a woman. We are men. There is nothing in the world that is able to trouble the mind of the philosopher."

"Nothing," said Mr. Emblem manfully, as if he, too, was a disciple. "Nothing; is there now?"

The stoutness of the assertion was sensibly impaired by the question.

"Not poverty, which is a shadow; nor pain, which passes; nor the loss of woman's love, which is a gain; nor fall from greatness—nothing. Nevertheless," his eyes did look anxious in spite of his philosophy, "this trouble of the child—will it soon be over?"

"I hope this evening," said Mr. Emblem. "Indeed I am sure that it will be finished this evening."

"If the child had a mother, or a brother, or any protectors but ourselves, my friend, we might leave her to them. But she has nobody except you and me. I am glad that she is not ill."

He left Mr. Emblem, and passing through the door of communication between house and shop, went noiselessly up the stairs.

One more visitor—unusual for so many to call on a September

afternoon. This time it was a youngish man of thirty or so, who stepped into the shop with an air of business, and, taking no notice at all of the assistant, walked swiftly into the back shop and shut the door behind him.

"I thought so," murmured Mr. James. "After he's been counting up his investments, his lawyer calls. More investments."

Mr. David Chalker was a solicitor and, according to his friends, who were proud of him, a sharp practitioner. He was, in fact, one of those members of the profession who, starting with no connection, have to make business for themselves. This, in London, they do by encouraging the county court, setting neighbors by the ears, lending money in small sums, fomenting quarrels, charging commissions, and generally making themselves a blessing and a boon to the district where they reside. But chiefly Mr. Chalker occupied himself with lending money.

"Now, Mr. Emblem," he said, not in a menacing tone, but as one who warns; "now, Mr. Emblem."

"Now, Mr. Chalker," the bookseller repeated mildly.

"What are you going to do for me?"

"I got your usual notice," the old bookseller began, hesitating, "six months ago."

"Of course you did. Three fifty is the amount. Three fifty, exactly."

"Just so. But I am afraid I am not prepared to pay off the bill of sale. The interest, as usual, will be ready."

"Of course it will. But this time the principal must be ready too."

"Can't you get another client to find the money?"

"No, I can't. Money is tight, and your security, Mr. Emblem, isn't so good as it was."

"The furniture is there, and so is the stock."

"Furniture wears out; as for the stock—who knows what that is worth? All your books together may not be worth fifty pounds, for what I know."

"Then what am I to do?"

"Find the money yourself. Come, Mr. Emblem, everybody knows—your grandson himself told me—all the world knows—you've been for years saving up for your grand-daughter. You told Joe only six months ago—you can't deny it—that whatever happened to you she would be well off."

Mr. Emblem did not deny the charge. But he ought not to have told this to his grandson, of all people in the world.

"As for Joe," Mr. Chalker went on, "you are going to do nothing for him. I know that. But is it business like, Mr. Emblem, to waste good money which you might have invested for your granddaughter?"

"You do not understand. Mr. Chalker. You really do not, and I cannot explain. But about this bill of sale—never mind my granddaughter."

"You the aforesaid Richard Emblem"—Mr. Chalker began to recite, without commas—"have assigned to me David Chalker aforesaid his executors administrators and assigns all and singular the several chattels and things specifically described in the schedule hereto annexed by way of security for the payment of the sum of three hundred and fifty pounds and interest thereon at the rate of eight per cent. per annum."

"Thank you, Mr. Chalker. I know all that."

"You can't complain, I'm sure. It is five years since you borrowed the money."

"It was fifty pounds and a box of old law books out of your office, and I signed a bill for a hundred."

"You forget the circumstances."

"No, I do not. My grandson was a rogue. One does not readily forget that circumstance. He was also your friend, I remember."

"And I held my tongue."

"I have had no more money from you, and the sum has become three hundred and fifty."

"Of course you don't understand law, Mr. Emblem. How should you! But we lawyers don't work for nothing. However it isn't what you got, but what I am to get. Come, my good sir, it's cutting off your nose to spite your face. Settle and have done with it, even if it does take a little slice off your granddaughter's fortune? Now look here"—his voice became persuasive—"why not take me into your confidence? Make a friend of me. You want advice; let me advise you. I can get you good investments—far better than you know anything of— good and safe investments—at six certain, and sometimes seven and even eight per cent. Make me your man of business—come now. As for this trumpery bill of sale—this trifle of three fifty, what is it to you? Nothing—nothing. And as for your intention to enrich your granddaughter, and cut off your grandson with a shilling, why I honor you for it—there, though he was my friend. For Joe deserves it thoroughly. I've told him so, mind. You ask him. I've told him so a dozen times. I've said: 'The old man's right, Joe.' Ask him if I haven't."

This was very expansive, but somehow Mr. Emblem did not respond.

Presently, however, he lifted his head.

"I have three weeks still."

"Three weeks still."

"And if I do not find the money within three weeks?"

"Why—but of course you will—but if you do not—I suppose there will be only one thing left to do—realize the security, sell up—sticks and books and all."

"Thank you, Mr. Chalker. I will look round me, and—and—do my best. Good day, Mr. Chalker."

"The best you can do, Mr. Emblem," returned the solicitor, "is to take me as your adviser. You trust David Chalker."

"Thank you. Good-day, Mr. Chalker."

On his way out, Mr. Chalker stopped for a moment and looked round the shop.

"How's business?" he asked the assistant.

"Dull, sir," replied Mr. James. "He throws it all away, and neglects his chances. Naturally, being so rich—"

"So rich, indeed," the solicitor echoed.

"It will be bad for his successor," Mr. James went on, thinking how much he should himself like to be that successor. "The goodwill won't be worth half what it ought to be, and the stock is just falling to pieces."

Mr. Chalker looked about him again thoughtfully, and opened his mouth as if about to ask a question, but said nothing. He remembered, in time, that the shopman was not likely to know the amount of his master's capital or investments.

"There isn't a book even in the glass-case that's worth a five-pound note," continued Mr. James, whispering, "and he don't look about for purchases any more. Seems to have lost his pluck."

Mr. Chalker returned to the back-shop.

"Within three weeks, Mr. Emblem," he repeated, and then departed.

Mr. Emblem sat in his chair. He had to find three hundred and fifty pounds in three weeks. No one knew better than himself that this was impossible. Within three weeks! But, in three weeks, he would open the packet of letters, and give Iris her inheritance. At least, she would not suffer. As for himself— He looked round the little back shop, and tried to recall the fifty years he had spent there, the books he had bought and sold, the money which had slipped through his fingers, the friends who had come and gone. Why, as for the books, he seemed to remember them every one—his joy in the purchase, his pride in possession, and his grief at letting them go. All the friends gone before him, his trade sunk to nothing.

"Yet," he murmured, "I thought it would last my time."

But the clock struck six. It was his tea-time. He rose mechanically, and went upstairs to Iris.

CHAPTER II

FOX AND WOLF

Mr. James, left to himself, attempted, in accordance with his daily custom, to commit a dishonorable action.

That is to say, he first listened carefully to the retreating footsteps of his master, as he went up the stairs; then he left his table, crept stealthily into the back shop, and began to pull the drawers, turn the handle of the safe, and try the desk. Everything was carefully locked. Then he turned over all the papers on the table, but found nothing that contained the information he looked for. It was his daily practice thus to try the locks, in hope that some day the safe, or the drawers, or the desk would be left open by accident, when he might be able to solve a certain problem, the doubt and difficulty of which sore let and hindered him—namely, of what extent, and where placed, were those great treasures, savings, and investments which enabled his master to be careless over his business. It was, further, customary with him to be thus frustrated and disappointed. Having briefly, therefore, also in accordance with his usual custom, expressed his disgust at this want of confidence between master and man, Mr. James returned to his paste and scissors.

About a quarter past six the shop door was cautiously opened, and a head appeared, which looked round stealthily. Seeing nobody about except Mr. James, the head nodded, and presently followed by its body, stepped into the shop.

"Where's the admiral, Foxy?" asked the caller.

"Guv'nor's upstairs, Mr. Joseph, taking of his tea with Miss Iris," replied Mr. James, not at all offended by the allusion to his craftiness. Who should resemble the fox if not the second-hand bookseller? In no trade, perhaps, can the truly admirable qualities of that animal—his patience, his subtlety and craft, his pertinacity, his sagacity—be illustrated more to advantage. Mr. James felt a glow of virtue—would that he could grow daily and hourly, and more and more toward the perfect fox. Then, indeed, and not till then would he be able to live truly up to his second-hand books.

"Having tea with Iris; well—"

The speaker looked as if it required some effort to receive this statement with resignation.

"He always does at six o'clock. Why shouldn't he?" asked Mr. James.

"Because, James, he spends the time in cockering up that gal whom he's ruined and spoiled—him and the old nigger between them—so that her mind is poisoned against her lawful relations, and nothing will content her but coming into all the old man's money, instead of going share and share alike, as a cousin should, and especially a she-cousin, while there's a biscuit left in the locker and a drop of rum in the cask."

"Ah!" said Mr. James with a touch of sympathy, called forth, perhaps, by mention of the rum, which is a favorite drink with second-hand booksellers' assistants.

"Nothing too good for her," the other went on; "the best of education, pianos to play upon, and nobody good enough for her to know. Not on visiting terms, if you please, with her neighbors; waiting for duchesses to call upon her. And what is she, after all? A miserable teacher!"

Mr. Joseph Gallop was a young man somewhere between twenty and thirty, tall, large-limbed, well set-up, and broad-shouldered. A young man who, at first sight, would seem eminently fitted to push his own fortunes. Also, at first sight, a remarkably handsome fellow, with straight, clear-cut features and light, curly hair. When he swung along the street, his round hat carelessly thrown back, and his handsome face lit up by the sun, the old women murmured a blessing upon his comely head—as they used to do, a long time ago, upon the comely and curly head of Absalom—and the young women looked meaningly at one another—as was also done in the case of Absalom—and the object of their admiration knew that they were saying to each other, in the feminine way, where a look is as good as a whisper, "There goes a handsome fellow." Those who knew him better, and had looked more closely into his face, said that his mouth was bad and his eyes shifty. The same opinion was held by the wiser sort as regards his character. For, on the one hand, some averred that to their certain knowledge Joe Gallop had shown himself a monster of ingratitude toward his grandfather, who had paid his debts and done all kinds of things for him; on the other hand there were some who thought he had been badly treated; and some said that no good would ever come of a young fellow who was never able to remain in the same situation more than a month or so; and others said that he had certainly been unfortunate, but that he was a quick and clever young man, who would some day find the kind of work that suited him, and then he would show everybody of what stuff he was composed. As for us, we have only to judge of him by his actions.

"Perhaps, Mr. Joseph," said Mr. James, "perhaps Miss Iris won't have all bequeathed to her?"

"Do you know anything?" Joe asked quickly. "Has he made a new will lately?"

"Not that I know of. But Mr. Chalker has been here off and on a good bit now."

"Ah! Chalker's a close one, too. Else he'd tell me, his old friend. Look here, Foxy," he turned a beaming and smiling face upon the assistant. "If you should see anything or find anything out, tell me, mind. And, remember, I'll make it worth your while."

Mr. James looked as it he was asking himself how Joseph could make it worth his while, seeing that he got nothing more from his grandfather, and by his own showing never would have anything more.

"It's only his will I'm anxious to know about; that, and where he's put away all his money. Think what a dreadful thing it would be for his heirs if he were to go and die suddenly, and none of us to know where his investments are. As for the shop, that is already disposed of, as I dare say you know."

"Disposed of? The shop disposed of! Oh, Lord!" The assistant turned pale. "Oh, Mr. Joseph," he asked earnestly, "what will become of the shop? And who is to have it?"

"I am to have it," Mr. Joseph replied calmly. This was the lie absolute, and he invented it very cleverly and at the right moment—a thing which gives strength and life to a lie, because he already suspected the truth and guessed the secret hope and ambition which possesses every ambitious assistant in this trade—namely, to get the succession. Mr. James looked upon himself as the lawful and rightful heir to the business. But sometimes he entertained grievous doubts, and now indeed his heart sunk into his boots. "I am to have it," Joe repeated.

"Oh, I didn't know. You are to have it, then? Oh!"

If Mr. James had been ten years younger, I think he would have burst into tears. But at the age of forty weeping no longer presents itself as a form of relief. It is more usual to seek consolation in a swear. He stammered, however, while he turned pale, and then red, and then pale again.

"Yes, quite proper, Mr. Joseph, I'm sure, and a most beautiful business may be made again here by one who understands the way. Oh, you are a lucky man, Mr. Joseph. You are indeed, sir, to get such a noble chance."

"The shop," Joe went on, "was settled—settled upon me, long ago." The verb "to settle" is capable of conveying large and vague impressions. "But after all, what's the good of this place to a sailor?"

"The good—the good of this place?" Mr. James's cheek flushed. "Why, to make money, to be sure—to coin money in. If I had this place to myself—why—why, in two years I would be making as much as two hundred a year. I would indeed."

"You want to make money. Bah! That's all you fellows think of. To sit in the back shop all day long and to sell moldy books! We jolly sailor boys know better than that, my lad."

There really was something nautical about the look of the man. He wore a black-silk tie, in a sailor's running-knot, the ends loose; his waistcoat was unbuttoned, and his coat was a kind of jacket; not to speak of his swinging walk and careless pose. In fact, he had been a sailor; he had made two voyages to India and back as assistant-purser, or purser's clerk, on board a P. and O. boat, but some disagreement with his commanding officer concerning negligence, or impudence, or drink, or laziness—he had been charged in different situations and at different times with all these vices, either together or separately—caused him to lose his rating on the ship's books. However, he brought away from his short nautical experience, and preserved, a certain nautical swagger, which accorded well with his appearance, and gave him a swashbuckler air, which made those who knew him well lament that he had not graced the Elizabethan era, when he might have become a gallant buccaneer, and so got himself shot through the head; or that he had not flourished under the reign of good Queen Anne, when he would probably have turned pirate and been hanged; or that, being born in the Victorian age, he had not gone to the Far West, where he would, at least, have had the chance of getting shot in a gambling-saloon.

"As for me, when I get the business," he continued, "I shall look about for some one to carry it on until I am able to sell it for what it will fetch. Books at a penny apiece all round, I suppose"—James gasped—"shop furniture thrown in"—James panted—"and the goodwill for a small lump sum." James wondered how far his own savings, and what he could borrow, might go toward that lump sum, and how much might "remain." "My grandfather, as you know, of course, is soon going to retire from business altogether." This was another lie absolute, as Mr. Emblem had no intention whatever of retiring.

"Soon, Mr. Joseph? He has never said a word to me about it."

"Very soon, now—sooner than you expect. At seventy-five, and with all his money, why should he go on slaving any longer? Very soon, indeed. Any day."

"Mr. Joseph," the assistant positively trembled with eagerness and apprehension.

"What is it, James? Did you really think that a man like me was going to sit in a back shop among these moldy volumes all day? Come, that's too good. You might have given me credit for being one cut above a counter, too. I am a gentleman, James, if you please; I am an officer and a gentleman."

He then proceeded to explain, in language that smacked something of the sea, that his ideas soared far above trade, which was, at best, a contemptible occupation, and quite unworthy of a gentleman, particularly an officer and a gentleman; and that his personal friends would never condescend even to formal acquaintance, not to speak of friendship, with trade. This discourse may be omitted. When one reads about such a man as Joe Gallop, when we are told how he looked and what he said and how he said it, with what gestures and in what tone, we feel as if it would be impossible for the simplest person in the world to be mistaken as to his real character. My friends, especially my young friends, so far from the discernment of character being easy, it is, on the contrary, an art most difficult, and very rarely attained. Nature's indications are a kind of handwriting the characters in which are known to few, so that, for instance, the quick, enquiring glance of an eye, in which one may easily read—who knows the character—treachery, lying, and deception, just as in the letter Beth was originally easily discerned the effigies of a house, may very easily pass unread by the multitude. The language, or rather the alphabet, is much less complicated than the cuneiform of the Medes and Persians, yet no one studies it, except women, most of whom are profoundly skilled in this lore, which makes them so fearfully and wonderfully wise. Thus it is easy for man to deceive his brother man, but not his sister woman. Again, most of us are glad to take everybody on his own statements; there are, or may be, we are all ready to acknowledge, with sorrow for erring humanity, somewhere else in the world, such things as pretending, swindling, acting a part, and cheating, but they do not and cannot belong to our own world. Mr. James, the assistant, very well knew that Mr. Emblem's grandson had already, though still young, as bad a record as could be desired by any; that he had been turned out of one situation after another; that his grandfather had long since refused to help him any more; that he was always to be found in the Broad Path which leadeth to destruction. When he had money he ran down that path as fast as his legs could carry him; when he had none, he only walked and wished he could run. But he never left it, and never wished to leave it. Knowing all this, the man accepted and believed every word of Joe's story. James believed it, because he hoped it. He listened respectfully to Joe's declamation on the meanness of trade, and then he rubbed his hands, and said humbly that he ventured to hope, when the sale of the business came on, Mr. Joseph would let him have a chance.

"You?" asked Joe. "I never thought of you. But why not? Why not, I say? Why not you as well as anybody else?"

"Nobody but me, Mr. Joseph, knows what the business is, and how it might be improved; and I could make arrangements for paying by regular instalments."

"Well, we'll talk about it when the time comes. I won't forget. Sailors, you know, can't be expected to understand the value of shops. Say, James, what does the commodore do all day?"

"Sits in there and adds up his investments."

"Always doing that—eh? Always adding 'em up? Ah, and you've never got a chance of looking over his shoulder, I suppose?"

"Never."

"You may find that chance, one of these days. I should like to know, if only for curiosity, what they are and where they are. He sits in there and adds 'em up. Yes—I've seen him at it. There must be thousands by this time."

"Thousands," said the assistant, in the belief that the more you add up a sum the larger it grows.

Joe walked into the back shop and tried the safe.

"Where are the keys?" he asked.

"Always in his pocket or on the table before him. He don't leave them about."

"Or you'd ha' known pretty sharp all there is to know—eh, my lad? Well, you're a foxy one, you are, if ever there was one. Let's be pals, you and me. When the old man goes, you want the shop—well, I don't see why you shouldn't have the shop. Somebody must have the shop; and it will be mine to do what I please with. As for his savings, he says they are all for Iris— well, wills have been set aside before this. Do you think now, seriously, do you think, James that the old man is quite right—eh? Don't answer in a hurry. Do you think, now, that he is quite right in his chump?"

James laughed.

"He's right enough, though he throws away his chances."

"Throws away his chances. How the deuce can he be all right then? Did you ever hear of a bookseller in his right mind throwing away his chances?"

"Why—no—for that matter—"

"Very well, then; for that matter, don't forget that you've seen him throw away all his chances—all his chances, you said. You are ready to swear to that. Most important evidence, that, James." James had not said "all," but he grunted, and the other man went on: "It may come in useful, this recollection. Keep your eyes wide-open, my red haired pirate. As for the moldy old shop, you may consider it as good as your own. Why, I suppose you'll get somebody else to handle the paste-brush and the scissors, and tie up the parcels, and water the shop—eh? You'll be too proud to do that for yourself, you will."

Mr. James grinned and rubbed his hands.

"All your own—eh? Well, you'll wake 'em up a bit, won't you?"

Mr. James grinned again—he continued grinning.

"Go on, Mr. Joseph," he said; "go on—I like it."

"Consider the job as settled, then. As for terms they shall be easy; I'm not a hard man. And—I say, Foxy, about that safe?"

Mr. James suddenly ceased grinning, because he observed a look in his patron's eyes which alarmed him.

"About that safe. You must find out for me where the old man has put his money, and what it is worth. Do you hear? Or else—"

"How can I find out? He won't tell me any more than you."

"Or else you must put me in the way of finding out." Mr. Joseph lowered his voice to a whisper. "He keeps the keys on the table before him. When a customer takes him out here, he leaves the keys behind him. Do you know the key of the safe?"

"Yes, I know it."

"What is to prevent a clever, quick-eyed fellow like you, mate, stepping in with a bit of wax—eh? While he is talking, you know. You could rush it in a moment."

"It's—it's dangerous, Mr. Joseph."

"So it is—rather dangerous—not much. What of that?"

"I would do anything I could to be of service to you, Mr. Joseph; but that's not honest, and it's dangerous."

"Dangerous! There's danger in the briny deep and shipwreck on the blast, if you come to danger. Do we, therefore, jolly mariners afloat ever think of that? Never. As to honesty, don't make a man sick."

"Look here, Mr. Joseph. If you'll give me a promise in writing, that I'm to have the shop, as soon as you get it, at a fair valuation and easy terms—say ten per cent down, and—"

"Stow it, mate; write what you like, and I'll sign it. Now about that key?"

"Supposing you was to get a duplicate key, and supposing you was to get into trouble about it, Mr. Joseph, should you— should you—I only put it to you—should you up and round upon the man as got you that key?"

"Foxy, you are as suspicious as a Chinaman. Well, then, do it this way. Send it me in a letter, and then who is to know where the letter came from?"

The assistant nodded.

"Then I think I can do the job, though not, perhaps, your way. But I think I can do it. I won't promise for a day or two."

"There you spoke like an honest pal and a friendly shipmate. Dangerous! Of course it is. When the roaring winds do blow— Hands upon it, brother. Foxy, you've never done a better day's work. You are too crafty for any sailor—you are, indeed. Here, just for a little key—"

"Hush, Mr. Joseph! Oh, pray—pray don't talk so loud! You don't know who may be listening. There's Mr. Lala Roy. You never hear him coming."

"Just for a trifle of a key, you are going to get possession of the best book-shop in all Chelsea. Well, keep your eyes skinned and the wax ready, will you? And now, James, I'll be off."

"Oh, I say, Mr. Joseph, wait a moment!" James was beginning to realize what he had promised. "If anything dreadful should come of this? I don't know what is in the safe. There may be money as well as papers."

"James, do you think I would steal? Do you mean to insinuate that I am a thief, sir? Do you dare to suspect that I would take money?"

James certainly looked as if he had thought even that possible.

"I shall open the safe, take out the papers, read them, and put them back just as I found them. Will that do for you?"

He shook hands again, and took himself off.

At seven o'clock Mr. Emblem came down-stairs again.

"Has any one been?" he asked as usual.

"Only Mr. Joseph."

"What might Mr. Joseph want?"

"Nothing at all."

"Then," said his grandfather, "Mr. Joseph might just as well have kept away."

*　*　*　*　*

Let us anticipate a little. James spent the next day hovering about in the hope that an opportunity would offer of getting the key in his possession for a few moments. There was no opportunity. The bunch of keys lay on the table under the old man's eyes all day, and when he left the table he carried them with him. But the day afterward he got his chance. One of the old customers called to talk over past bargains and former prizes. Mr. Emblem came out of the back shop with his visitor, and continued talking with him as far as the door. As he passed the table—James's table—he rested the hand which carried the keys on it, and left them there. James pounced upon them and slipped them into his pocket noiselessly. Mr. Emblem returned to his own chair and thought nothing of the keys for an hour and a half by the clock, and during this period James was out on business. When Mr. Emblem remembered his keys, he felt for them in their usual place and missed them, and then began searching about and cried out to James that he had lost his bunch of keys.

"Why, sir," said James, bringing them to him, after a little search, and with a very red face, "here they are; you must have left them on my table."

And in this way the job was done.

CHAPTER III

IRIS THE HERALD

By a somewhat remarkable coincidence it was on this very evening that Iris first made the acquaintance of her pupil, Mr. Arnold Arbuthnot. These coincidences, I believe, happen oftener in real life than they do even on the stage, where people are always turning up at the very nick of time and the critical moment.

I need little persuasion to make me believe that the first meeting of Arnold Arbuthnot and Iris, on the very evening when her cousin was opening matters with the Foxy one, was nothing short of Providential. You shall see, presently, what things might have happened if they had not met. The meeting was, in fact, the second of the three really important events in the life of a girl. The first, which is seldom remembered with the gratitude which it deserves, is her birth; the second, the first meeting with her future lover; the third, her wedding-day; the other events of a woman's life are interesting, perhaps, but not important.

Certain circumstances, which will be immediately explained, connected with this meeting, made it an event of very considerable interest to Iris, even though she did not suspect its immense importance. So much interest that she thought of nothing else for a week beforehand; that as the appointed hour drew near she trembled and grew pale; that when her grandfather came up for his tea, she, who was usually so quick to discern the least sign of care or anxiety in his face, actually did not observe the trouble, plainly written in his drooping head and anxious eyes, which was due to his interview with Mr. David Chalker.

She poured out the tea, therefore, without one word of sympathy. This would have seemed hard if her grandfather had expected any. He did not, however, because he did not know that the trouble showed in his face, and was trying to look as if nothing had happened. Yet in his brain were ringing and resounding the words, "Within three weeks—within three weeks," with the regularity of a horrid clock at midnight, when one wants to go to sleep.

"Oh," cried Iris, forced, as young people always are, to speak of her own trouble, "oh, grandfather, he is coming to-night."

"Who is coming to-night, my dear?" and then he listened again for the ticking of the clock: "Within three weeks—within three weeks." "Who is coming to-night, my dear?"

He took the cup of tea from her, and sat down with an old man's deliberation, which springs less from wisdom and the fullness of thought that from respect to rheumatism.

The iteration of that refrain, "Within three weeks," made him forget everything, even the trouble of his granddaughter's mind.

"Oh, grandfather, you cannot have forgotten!"

She spoke with the least possible touch of irritation, because she had been thinking of this thing for a week past, day and night, and it was a thing of such stupendous interest to her, that it seemed impossible that anyone who knew of it could forget what was coming.

"No, no." The old man was stimulated into immediate recollection by the disappointment in her eyes. "No, no, my dear, I have not forgotten. Your pupil is coming. Mr. Arbuthnot is coming. But, Iris, child, don't let that worry you. I will see him for you, if you like."

"No; I must see him myself. You see, dear, there is the awful deception. Oh, how shall I tell him?"

"No deception at all," he said stoutly. "You advertised in your own initials. He never asked if the initials belonged to a man or to a woman. The other pupils do not know. Why should this one? What does it matter to him if you have done the work for which he engaged your services?"

"But, oh, he is so different! And the others, you know, keep to the subject."

"So should he, then. Why didn't he?"

"But he hasn't. And I have been answering him, and he must think that I was drawing him on to tell me more about himself; and now—oh, what will he think? I drew him on and on—yet I didn't mean to—till at last he writes to say that he regards me as the best friend and the wisest adviser he has ever had. What will he think and say? Grandfather, it is dreadful!"

"What did you tell him for, Iris, my dear? Why couldn't you let things go on? And by telling him you will lose your pupil."

"Yes, of course; and, worse still, I shall lose his letters. We live so quietly here that his letters have come to me like news of another world. How many different worlds are there all round one in London? It has been pleasant to read of that one in which ladies go about beautifully dressed always, and where the people have nothing to do but to amuse themselves. He has told me about this world in which he lives, and about his own life, so that I know everything he does, and where he goes; and"—here she sighed heavily—"of course it could not go on forever; and I should not mind so much if it had not been carried on under false pretenses."

"No false pretenses at all, my dear. Don't think it."

"I sent back his last check," she said, trying to find a little consolation for herself. "But yet—"

"Well, Iris," said her grandfather, "he wanted to learn heraldry, and you have taught him."

"For the last three months"—the girl blushed as if she was confessing her sins—"for the last three months there has not been a single word in his letters about heraldry. He tells me that he writes because he is idle, or because he wants to talk, or because he is alone in his studio, or because he wants his unknown friend's advice. I am his unknown friend, and I have been giving him advice."

"And very good advice, too," said her grandfather benevolently. "Who is so wise as my Iris?"

"I have answered all his letters, and never once told him that I am only a girl."

"I am glad you did not tell him, Iris," said her grandfather; but he did not say why he was glad. "And why can't he go on writing his letters without making any fuss?"

"Because he says he must make the acquaintance of the man— the man, he says—with whom he has been in correspondence so long. This is what he says."

She opened a letter which lay upon a table covered with papers, but her grandfather stopped her.

"Well, my dear, I do not want to know what he says. He wishes to make your acquaintance. Very good, then. You are going to see him, and to tell him who you are. That is enough. But as for deceiving"—he paused, trying to understand this extreme scrupulosity of conscience—"if you come to deceiving—well, in a kind sort of a way you did allow him to think his correspondent a man. I admit that. What harm is done to him? None. He won't be so mean, I suppose, as to ask for his money back again."

"I think he ought to have it all back," said Iris; "yes, all from the very beginning. I am ashamed that I ever took any money from him. My face burns when I think of it."

To this her grandfather made no reply. The returning of money paid for services rendered was, to his commercial mind, too foolish a thing to be even talked about. At the same time, Iris was quite free to manage her own affairs. And then there was that roll of papers in the safe. Why, what matter if she sent away all her pupils? He changed the subject.

"Iris, my dear," he said, "about this other world, where the people amuse themselves; the world which lives in the squares and in the big houses on the Chelsea Embankment here, you know—how should you like, just for a change, to belong to that world and have no work to do?"

"I don't know," she replied carelessly, because the question did not interest her.

"You would have to leave me, of course. You would sever your connection, as they say, with the shop."

"Please, don't let us talk nonsense, grandfather."

"You would have to be ashamed, perhaps, of ever having taught for your living."

"Now that I never should be—never, not if they made me a duchess."

"You would go dressed in silk and velvet. My dear, I should like to see you dressed up just for once, as we have seen them at the theater."

"Well, I should like one velvet dress in my life. Only one. And it should be crimson—a beautiful, deep, dark crimson."

"Very good. And you would drive in a carriage instead of an omnibus; you would sit in the stalls instead of the upper circle; you would give quantities of money to poor people; and you would buy as many second hand books as you pleased. There are rich people, I believe, ostentatious people, who buy new books. But you, my dear, have been better brought up. No books are worth buying till they have stood the criticism of a whole generation at least. Never buy new books, my dear."

"I won't," said Iris. "But, you dear old man, what have you got in your head to-night? Why in the world should we talk about getting rich?"

"I was only thinking," he said, "that perhaps, you might be so much happier—"

"Happier? Nonsense! I am as happy as I can be. Six pupils already. To be sure I have lost one," she sighed; "and the best among them all."

When her grandfather left her, Iris placed candles on the writing-table, but did not light them, though it was already pretty dark. She had half an hour to wait; and she wanted to think, and candles are not necessary for meditation. She sat at the open window and suffered her thoughts to ramble where they pleased. This is a restful thing to do, especially if your windows look upon a tolerably busy but not noisy London road. For then, it is almost as good as sitting beside a swiftly-running stream; the movement of the people below is like the unceasing flow of the current; the sound of the footsteps is like the whisper of the water along the bank; the echo of the half heard talk strikes your ear like the mysterious voices wafted to the banks from the boats as they go by; and the lights of the shops and the street presently become spectral and unreal like lights seen upon the river in the evening.

Iris had a good many pupils—six, in fact, as she had boasted; why, then, was she so strangely disturbed on account of one?

An old tutor by correspondence may be, and very likely is, indifferent about his pupils, because he has had so many; but Iris was a young tutor, and had as yet known few. One of her pupils, for instance, was a gentleman in the fruit and potato line, in the Borough. By reason of his early education, which had not been neglected so much as entirely omitted, he was unable to personally conduct his accounts. Now a merchant without his accounts is as helpless as a tourist without his Cook. So that he desired, in his mature age, to learn book keeping, compound addition, subtraction, and multiplication. He had no partners, so that he did not want division. But it is difficult—say, well-nigh impossible—for a middle-aged merchant, not trained in the graces of letter-writing, to inspire a young lady with personal regard, even though she is privileged to follow the current of his thoughts day by day, and to set him his sums.

Next there was a young fellow of nineteen or twenty, who was beginning life as an assistant-teacher in a commercial school at Lower Clapton. This way is a stony and a thorny path to tread; no one walks upon it willingly; those who are compelled to enter upon it speedily either run away and enlist, or they go and find a secluded spot in which to hang themselves. The smoother ways of the profession are only to be entered by one who is the possessor of a degree, and it was the determination of this young man to pass the London University Examinations, and to obtain the degree of Bachelor. In this way his value in the educational market would be at once doubled, and he could command a better place and lighter work. He showed himself, in his letters, to be an eminently practical, shrewd, selfish, and thick-skinned young man, who would quite certainly get on in the world, and was resolved to lose no opportunities, and, with that view, he took as much work out of his tutor as he could get for the money. Had he known that the "I.A." who took such a wonderful amount of trouble with his papers was only a woman, he would certainly have extorted a great deal more work for his money. All this Iris read in his letters and understood. There is no way in which a man more surely and more naturally reveals his true character than in his correspondence, so that after awhile, even though the subject of the letters be nothing more interesting than the studies in hand, those who write the letters may learn to know each other if they have but the mother wit to read between the lines. Certainly this young schoolmaster did not know Iris, nor did he desire to discover what she was like, being wholly occupied with the study of himself. Strange and kindly provision of Nature. The less desirable a man actually appears to others, the more fondly he loves and believes in himself. I have heard it whispered that Narcissus was a hunchback.

Then there was another pupil, a girl who was working her very hardest in order to become, as she hoped, a first-class governess, and who, poor thing! by reason of her natural thickness would never reach even the third rank. Iris would have been sorry for her, because she worked so fiercely, and was so stupid, but there was something hard and unsympathetic in her nature which forbade pity. She was miserably poor, too, and had an unsuccessful father, no doubt as stupid as herself, and made pitiful excuses for not forwarding the slender fees with regularity.

Everybody who is poor should be, on that ground alone, worthy of pity and sympathy. But the hardness and stupidity, and the ill-temper, all combined and clearly shown in her letters, repelled her tutor. Iris, who drew imaginary portraits of her pupils, pictured the girl as plain to look upon, with a dull eye, a leathery, pallid cheek, a forehead without sunshine upon it, and lips which seldom parted with a smile.

Then there was, besides, a Cambridge undergraduate. He was neither clever, nor industrious, nor very ambitious; he thought that a moderate place was quite good enough for him to aim at, and he found that his unknown and obscure tutor by correspondence was cheap and obliging, and willing to take trouble, and quite as efficacious for his purposes as the most expensive Cambridge coach. Iris presently discovered that he was lazy and luxurious, a deceiver of himself, a dweller in Fool's Paradise and a constant shirker of work. Therefore, she disliked him. Had she actually known him and talked with him, she might have liked him better in spite of these faults and shortcomings, for he was really a pleasant, easygoing youth, who wallowed in intellectual sloth, but loved physical activity; who will presently drop easily, and comfortably, and without an effort or a doubt, into the bosom of the Church, and will develop later on into an admirable country parson, unless they disestablish the Establishment: in which case, I do not know what he will do.

But this other man, this man who was coming for an explanation, this Mr. Arnold Arbuthnot, was, if you please, a very different kind of pupil. In the first place he was a gentleman, a fact which he displayed, not ostentatiously, in every line of his letters; next, he had come to her for instruction—the only pupil she had in that science, in heraldry, which she loved. It is far more pleasant to be describing a shield and settling questions in the queer old language of this queer old science, than in solving and propounding problems in trigonometry and conic sections. And then—how if your pupil begins to talk round the subject and to wander into other things? You cannot very well talk round a branch of mathematics, but heraldry is a subject surrounded by fields, meadows, and lawns, so to speak, all covered with beautiful flowers. Into these the pupil wandered, and Iris not unwillingly followed. Thus the teaching of heraldry by correspondence became the most delightful interchange of letters imaginable, set off and enriched with a curious and strange piquancy, derived from the fact that one of them, supposed to be an elderly man, was a young girl, ignorant of the world except from books, and the advice given her by two old men, who formed all her society. Then, as was natural, what was at first a kind of play, became before long a serious and earnest confidence on the one side, and a hesitating reception on the other.

Latterly he more than once amused himself by drawing an imaginary portrait of her; it was a pleasing portrait, but it made her feel uneasy.

"I know you," he said, "from your letters, but yet I want to know you in person. I think you are a man advanced in years." Poor Iris! and she not yet twenty-one. "You sit in your study and read; you wear glasses, and your hair is gray; you have a kind heart and a cheerful voice; you are not rich—you have never tried to make yourself rich; you are therefore little versed in the ways of mankind; you take your ideas chiefly from books; the few friends you have chosen are true and loyal; you are full of sympathy, and quick to read the thoughts of those in whom you take an interest." A very fine character, but it made Iris's cheek to burn and her eyes to drop. To be sure she was not rich, nor did she know the world; so far her pupil was right, but yet she was not gray nor old. And, again, she was not, as he thought, a man.

Letter-writing is not extinct, as it is a commonplace to affirm, and as people would have us believe. Letters are written still— the most delightful letters—letters as copious, as charming, as any of the last century; but men and women no longer write their letters as carefully as they used to do in the old days, because they were then shown about, and very likely read aloud. Our letters, therefore, though their sentences are not so balanced nor their periods so rounded, are more real, more truthful, more spontaneous, and more delightful than the laborious productions of our ancestors, who had to weigh every phrase, and to think out their bon mots, epigrams, and smart things for weeks beforehand, so that the letter might appear full of impromptu wit. I should like, for instance, just for once, to rob the outward or the homeward mail, in order to read all the delightful letters which go every week backward and forward between the folk in India and the folk at home.

"I shall lose my letters," Iris recollected, and her heart sunk. Not only did her correspondent begin to draw these imaginary portraits of her, but he proceeded to urge upon her to come out of her concealment, and to grant him an interview. This she might have refused, in her desire to continue a correspondence which brightened her monotonous life. But there came another thing, and this decided her. He began to give, and to ask, opinions concerning love, marriage, and such topics—and then she perceived it could not possibly be discussed with him, even in domino and male disguise. "As for love," her pupil wrote, "I suppose it is a real and not a fancied necessity of life. A man, I mean, may go on a long time without it, but there will come a time—do not you think so?—when he is bound to feel the incompleteness of life without a woman to love. We ought to train our boys and girls from the very beginning to regard love and marriage as the only things really worth having, because without them there is no happiness. Give me your own experience. I am sure you must have been in love at some time or other in your life."

Anybody will understand that Iris could not possibly give her own experience in love-matters, nor could she plunge into speculative philosophy of this kind with her pupil. Obviously the thing must come to an end. Therefore she wrote a letter to him, telling him that "I.A." would meet him, if he pleased, that very evening at the hour of eight.

It is by this time sufficiently understood that Iris Aglen professed to teach—it is an unusual combination—mathematics and heraldry; she might also have taught equally well, had she chosen, sweetness of disposition, goodness of heart, the benefits conferred by pure and lofty thoughts on the expression of a girl's face, and the way to acquire all the other gracious, maidenly virtues; but either there is too limited a market for these branches of culture, or—which is perhaps the truer reason—there are so many English girls, not to speak of Americans, who are ready and competent to teach them, and do teach them to their brothers, and their lovers, and to each other, and to their younger sisters all day long.

As for her heraldry, it was natural that she should acquire that science, because her grandfather knew as much as any

Pursuivant or King-at-Arms, and thought that by teaching the child a science which is nowadays cultivated by so few, he was going to make her fortune. Besides, ever mindful of the secret packet, he thought that an heiress ought to understand heraldry. It was, indeed, as you shall see, in this way that her fortune was made; but yet not quite in the way he proposed to make it. Nobody ever makes a fortune quite in the way at first intended for him.

As for her mathematics, it is no wonder that she was good in this science, because she was a pupil of Lala Roy.

This learned Bengalee condescended to acknowledge the study of mathematics as worthy even of the Indian intellect, and amused himself with them when he was not more usefully engaged in chess. He it was who, being a lodger in the house, taught Iris almost as soon as she could read how letters placed side by side may be made to signify and accomplish stupendous things, and how they may disguise the most graceful and beautiful curves, and how they may even open a way into boundless space, and there disclose marvels. This wondrous world did the philosopher open to the ready and quick-witted girl; nor did he ever lead her to believe that it was at all an unusual or an extraordinary thing for a girl to be so quick and apt for science as herself, nor did he tell her that if she went to Newnham or to Girton, extraordinary glories would await her, with the acclamations of the multitude in the Senate House and the praise of the Moderators. Iris, therefore, was not proud of her mathematics, which seemed part of her very nature. But of her heraldry she was, I fear, extremely proud—proud even to sinfulness. No doubt this was the reason why, through her heraldry, the humiliation of this evening fell upon her.

"If he is young," she thought, "if he is young—and he is sure to be young—he will be very angry at having opened his mind to a girl"—it will be perceived that, although she knew so much mathematics, she was really very ignorant of the opposite sex, not to know that a young man likes nothing so much as the opening of his mind to a young lady. "If he is old, he will be more humiliated still"—as if any man at any age was ever humiliated by confessing himself to a woman. "If he is a proud man, he will never forgive me. Indeed, I am sure that he can never forgive me, whatever kind of man he is. But I can do no more than tell him I am sorry. If he will not forgive me then, what more can I say? Oh, if he should be vindictive!"

When the clock began to strike the hour of eight, Iris lighted her candles, and before the pulsation of the last stroke had died away, she heard the ringing of the house-bell.

The door was opened by her grandfather himself, and she heard his voice.

"Yes," he said, "you will find your tutor, in the first floor front, alone. If you are inclined to be vindictive, when you hear all, please ring the bell for me."

The visitor mounted the stairs, and Iris, hearing his step, began to tremble and to shake for fear.

When the door opened she did not at first look up. But she knew that her pupil was there, and that he was looking for his tutor.

"Pardon me"—the voice was not unpleasant—"pardon me. I was directed to this room. I have an appointment with my tutor."

"If," said Iris, rising, for the time for confession had at length arrived, "if you are Mr. Arnold Arbuthnot, your appointment is, I believe, with me."

"It is with my tutor," he said.

"I am your tutor. My initials are I.A."

The room was only lighted by two candles, but they showed

him the hanging head and the form of a woman, and he thought she looked young, judging by the outline. Her voice was sweet and clear.

"My tutor? You?"

"If you really are Mr. Arnold Arbuthnot, the gentleman who has corresponded with I.A. for the last two years on heraldry, and—and other things, I am your tutor."

She had made the dreaded confession. The rest would be easy. She even ventured to raise her eyes, and she perceived, with a sinking of the heart, that her estimate of her pupil's age was tolerably correct. He was a young man, apparently not more than five or six and twenty.

It now remained to be seen if he was vindictive.

As for the pupil, when he recovered a little from the blow of this announcement, he saw before him a girl, quite young, dressed in a simple gray or drab colored stuff, which I have reason to believe is called Carmelite. The dress had a crimson kerchief arranged in folds over the front, and a lace collar, and at first sight it made the beholder feel that, considered merely as a setting of face and figure, it was remarkably effective. Surely this is the true end and aim of all feminine adornment, apart from the elementary object of keeping one warm.

"I—I did not know," the young man said, after a pause, "I did not know at all that I was corresponding with a lady."

Here she raised her eyes again, and he observed that the eyes were very large and full of light—"eyes like the fishpools of Heshbon"—dove's eyes.

"I am very sorry," she said meekly. "It was my fault."

He observed other things now, having regained the use of his senses. Thus he saw that she wore her hair, which was of a wonderful chestnut brown color, parted at the side like a boy's, and that she had not committed the horrible enormity of cutting it short. He observed, too, that while her lips were quivering and her cheek was blushing, her look was steadfast. Are dove's eyes, he asked himself, always steadfast?

"I ought to have told you long ago, when you began to write about—about yourself and other things, when I understood that you thought I was a man—oh, long ago I ought to have told you the truth!"

"It is wonderful!" said the young man, "it is truly wonderful!" He was thinking of the letters—long letters, full of sympathy, and a curious unworldly wisdom, which she had sent him in reply to his own, and he was comparing them with her youthful face, as one involuntarily compares a poet's appearance with his poetry—generally a disappointing thing to do, and always a foolish thing.

"I am very sorry," she repeated.

"Have you many pupils, like myself?"

"I have several pupils in mathematics. It does not matter to them whether they are taught by a man or a woman. In heraldry I had only one—you."

He looked round the room. One end was occupied by shelves, filled with books; in one of the windows was a table, covered with papers and adorned with a type-writer, by means of which Iris carried on her correspondence. For a moment the unworthy thought crossed his mind that he had been, perhaps, artfully lured on by a siren for his destruction. Only for a moment, however, because she raised her face and met his gaze again, with eyes so frank and innocent, that he could not doubt them. Besides, there was the clear outline of her face, so truthful and so honest. The young man was an artist, and therefore believed in outline. Could any sane and intelligent creature doubt those curves of cheek and chin?

Walter Besant

"I have put together," she said, "all your letters for you. Here they are. Will you, please, take them back? I must not keep them any longer." He took them, and bowed. "I made this appointment, as you desired, to tell you the truth, because I have deceived you too long: and to beg you to forgive me; and to say that, of course, there is an end to our correspondence."

"Thank you. It shall be as you desire. Exactly," he repeated, "as you desire."

He ought to have gone at once. There was nothing more to say. Yet he lingered, holding the letters in his hand.

"To write these letters," he said, "has been for a long time one of my greatest pleasures, partly because I felt that I was writing to a friend, and so wrote in full trust and confidence; partly because they procured me a reply—in the shape of your letters. Must I take back these letters of mine?"

She made no answer.

"It is hard, is it not, to lose a friend so slowly acquired, thus suddenly and unexpectedly?"

"Yes," she said, "it is hard. I am very sorry. It was my fault."

"Perhaps I have said something, in my ignorance—something which ought not to have been said or written—something careless—something which has lowered me in your esteem—"

"Oh, no—no!" said Iris quickly. "You have never said anything that a gentleman should not have said."

"And if you yourself found any pleasure in answering my letters—"

"Yes," said Iris with frankness, "it gave me great pleasure to read and to answer your letters, as well as I could."

"I have not brought back your letters. I hope you will allow me to keep them. And, if you will, why should we not continue our correspondence as before?" But he did not ask the question confidently.

"No," said Iris decidedly "it can never be continued as before. How could it, when once we have met, and you have learned the truth?"

"Then," he continued, "if we cannot write to each other any more, can we not talk?"

She ought to have informed him on the spot that the thing was quite impossible, and not to be thought of for one moment. She should have said, coldly, but firmly—every right-minded and well-behaved girl would have said—"Sir, it is not right that you should come alone to a young lady's study. Such things are not to be permitted. It we meet in society, we may, perhaps, renew our acquaintance."

But girls do go on sometimes as if there was no such thing as propriety at all, and such cases are said to be growing more frequent. Besides, Iris was not a girl who was conversant with social convenances. She looked at her pupil thoughtfully and frankly.

"Can we?" she asked. She who hesitates is lost, a maxim which cannot be too often read, said, and studied. It is one of the very few golden rules omitted from Solomon's Proverbs. "Can we? It would be pleasant."

"It you will permit me," he blushed and stammered, wondering at her ready acquiescence, "if you will permit me to call upon you sometimes—here, if you will allow me, or anywhere else. You know my name. I am by profession an artist, and I have a studio close at hand in Tite Street."

"To call upon me here?" she repeated.

Now, when one is a tutor, and has been reading with a pupil for two years, one regards that pupil with a feeling which may not be exactly parental, but which is unconventional. If Arnold had said, "Behold me! May I, being a young man, call upon you, a young woman?" she would have replied: "No, young man, that can never be." But when he said, "May I, your pupil, call sometimes upon you, my tutor?" a distinction was at once established by which the impossible became possible.

"Yes," she said, "I think you may call. My grandfather has his tea with me every evening at six. You may call then if it will give you any pleasure."

"You really will let me come here?"

The young man looked as if the permission was likely to give him the greatest pleasure.

"Yes; if you wish it."

She spoke just exactly like an Oxford Don giving an undergraduate permission to take an occasional walk with him, or to call for conversation and advice at certain times in his rooms. Arnold noticed the manner, and smiled.

"Still," he said, "as your pupil."

He meant to set her at her ease concerning the propriety of these visits. She thought he meant a continuation of a certain little arrangement as to fees, and blushed.

"No," she said; "I must not consider you as a pupil any longer. You have put an end to that yourself."

"I do not mind, if only I continue your friend."

"Oh," she said, "but we must not pledge ourselves rashly to friendship. Perhaps you will not like me when you once come to know me."

"Then I remain your disciple."

"Oh no," she flushed again, "you must already think me presumptuous enough in venturing to give you advice. I have written so many foolish things—"

"Indeed, no," he interrupted, "a thousand times no. Let me tell you once for all, if I may, that you have taught me a great deal—far more than you can ever understand, or than I can explain. Where did you getyour wisdom? Not from the Book of Human Life. Of that you cannot knowmuch as yet."

"The wisdom is in your imagination, I think. You shall not be my pupil nor my disciple, but—well—because you have told me so much, and I seem to have known you so long, and, besides, because you must never feel ashamed of having told me so much, you shall come, if you please, as my brother."

It was not till afterward that she reflected on the vast responsibilities she incurred in making this proposal, and on the eagerness with which her pupil accepted it.

"As your brother!" he cried, offering her his hand. "Why, it is far—far more than I could have ventured to hope. Yes, I will come as your brother. And now, although you know so much about me, you have told me nothing about yourself—not even your name."

"My name is Iris Aglen."

"Iris! It is a pretty name!"

"It was, I believe, my grandmother's. But I never saw her, and I do not know who or what my father's relations are."

"Iris Aglen!" he repeated. "Iris was the Herald of the Gods, and the rainbow was constructed on purpose to serve her for a way from Heaven to the Earth."

"Mathematicians do not allow that," said the girl, smiling.

"I don't know any mathematics. But now I understand in what school you learned your heraldry. You are Queen-at-Arms at least, and Herald to the Gods of Olympus."

He wished to add something about the loveliness of Aphrodite, and the wisdom of Athene, but he refrained, which was in good taste.

"Thank you, Mr. Arbuthnot," Iris replied. "I learned my heraldry of my grandfather, who taught himself from the books he sells. And my mathematics I learned of Lala Roy, who is our lodger, and a learned Hindoo gentleman. My father is dead—and my mother as well—and I have no friends in the world except these two old men, who love me, and have done their best to spoil me."

Her eyes grew humid and her voice trembled.

No other friends in the world! Strange to say, this young man felt a little sense of relief. No other friends. He ought to have sympathized with the girl's loneliness; he might have asked her how she could possibly endure life without companionship, but he did not; he only felt that other friends might have been rough and ill-bred; this girl derived her refinement, not only from nature, but also from separation from the other girls who might in the ordinary course have been her friends and associates. And if no other friends, then no lover. Arnold was only going to visit the young lady as her brother; but lovers do not generally approve the introduction of such novel effects as that caused by the appearance of a brand-new and previously unsuspected brother. He was glad, on the whole, that there was no lover.

Then he left her, and went home to his studio, where he sat till midnight, sketching a thousand heads one after the other with rapid pencil. They were all girls' heads, and they all had hair parted on the left side, with a broad, square forehead, full eyes, and straight, clear-cut features.

"No," he said, "it is no good. I cannot catch the curve of her mouth—nobody could. What a pretty girl! And I am to be her brother! What will Clara say? And how—oh, how in the world can she be, all at the same time, so young, so pretty, so learned, so quick, so sympathetic, and so wise?"

CHAPTER IV

THE WOLF AT HOME

There is a certain music-hall, in a certain street, leading out of a certain road, and this is quite clear and definite enough. Its distinctive characteristics, above any of its fellows, is a vulgarity so profound, that the connoisseur or student in that branch of mental culture thinks that here at last he has reached the lowest depths. For this reason one shrinks from actually naming it, because it might become fashionable, and then, if it fondly tried to change its character to suit its changed audience, it might entirely lose its present charm, and become simply commonplace.

Joe Gallop stood in the doorway of this hall, a few days after the Tempting of Mr. James. It was about ten o'clock, when the entertainments were in full blast. He had a cigarette between his lips, as becomes a young man of fashion, but it had gone out, and he was thinking of something. To judge from the cunning look in his eyes, it was something not immediately connected with the good of his fellow-creatures. Presently the music of the orchestra ceased, and certain female acrobats, who had been "contorting" themselves fearfully and horribly for a quarter of an hour upon the stage, kissed their hands, which were as hard as ropes, from the nature of their profession, and smiled a fond farewell. There was some applause, but not much, because neither man nor woman cares greatly for female acrobats, and the performers themselves are with difficulty persuaded to learn their art, and generally make haste to "go in" again as soon as they can, and try henceforward to forget that they have ever done things with ropes and bars.

Joe, when they left the stage, ceased his meditations, whatever may have been their subject, lit a fresh cigarette, and assumed an air of great expectation, as if something really worth seeing and hearing were now about to appear. And when the chairman brought down the hammer with the announcement that Miss Carlotta Claradine, the People's Favorite, would now oblige, it was Joe who loudly led the way for a tumultuous burst of applause. Then the band, which at this establishment, and others like unto it, only plays two tunes, one for acrobats, and one for singers, struck up the second air, and the People's Favorite appeared. She may have had by nature a sweet and tuneful voice; perhaps it was in order to please her friends, the people, that, she converted it into a harsh and rasping voice, that she delivered her words with even too much gesture, and that she uttered a kind of shriek at the beginning of every verse, which was not in the composer's original music, but was thrown in to compel attention. She was dressed with great simplicity, in plain frock, apron, and white cap, to represent a fair young Quakeress, and she sung a song about her lover with much "archness"—a delightful quality in woman.

"Splendid, splendid! Bravo!" shouted Joseph at the end of the first verse. "That fetches 'em, don't it, sir? Positively drags 'em, in, sir."

He addressed his words, without turning his head, to a man who had just come in, and was gazing at him with unbounded astonishment.

"You here, Joe??" he said.

Joe started.

"Why, Chalker, who'd have thought to meet you in this music-hall?"

"It's a good step, isn't it? And what are you doing, Joe? I heard you'd left the P. and O. Company."

"Had to," said Joe. "A gentleman has no choice but to resign. Ought never to have gone there. There's no position, Chalker—no position at all in the service. That is what I felt. Besides, the uniform, for a man of my style, is unbecoming. And the captain was a cad."

"Humph! and what are you doing then? Living on the old man again?"

"Never you mind, David Chalker," replied Joe with dignity; "I am not likely to trouble you any more after the last time I called upon you."

"Well, Joe," said the other, without taking offense, "it is not my business to lend money without a security, and all you had to offer was your chance of what your grandfather might leave you—or might not."

"And a very good security too, if he does justice to his relations."

"Yes; but how did I know whether he was going to do justice? Come, Joe, don't be shirty with an old friend."

There was a cordiality in the solicitor's manner which boded well. Joe was pretty certain that Mr. Chalker was not a man to cultivate friendship unless something was to be got out of it. It is only the idle and careless who can waste time over unprofitable friendships. With most men friendship means assisting in each other's little games, so that every man must become, on occasion, bonnet, confederate, and pal, for his friend, and may expect the same kindly office for himself.

If Chalker wished to keep up his old acquaintance with Joe Gallop, there must be some good reason. Now the only reason which suggested itself to Joe at that moment was that Chalker had lately drawn a new will for the old man, and that he himself might be in it. Here he was wrong. The only reason of Mr. Chalker's friendly attitude was curiosity to know what Joe was doing, and how he was living.

"Look here, Chalker," Joe whispered, "you used to pretend to be a pal. What's the good of being a pal if you won't help a fellow? You see my grandfather once a week or so; you shut the door and have long talks with him. If you know what he's going to do with his money, why not tell a fellow? Let's make a business matter of it."

"How much do you know, Joe, and what is your business proposal worth?"

"Nothing at all; that's the honest truth—I know nothing. The old man's as tight as wax. But there's other business in the world besides his. Suppose I know of something a precious sight better than his investments, and suppose—just suppose—that I wanted a lawyer to manage it for me?"

"Well, Joe?"

"Encore! Bravo! Encore! Bravo!" Joe banged his stick on the floor and shouted because the singer ended her first song. He looked so fierce and big, that all the bystanders made haste to follow his example.

"Splendid, isn't she?" he said.

"Hang the singer! What do you mean by other business?"

"Perhaps it's nothing. Perhaps there will be thousands in it. And perhaps I can get on without you, after all."

"Very well, Joe. Get on without me if you like."

"Look here, Chalker," Joe laid a persuasive hand on the other's arm, "can't we two be friendly? Why don't you give a fellow a

Walter Besant

lift? All I want to know is where the old man's put his money, and how he's left it."

"Suppose I do know," Mr. Chalker replied, wishing ardently that he did, "do you think I am going to betray trust—a solicitor betray trust—and for nothing? But if you want to talk real business, Joe, come to my office. You know where that is."

Joe knew very well; in fact, there had been more than one difficulty which had been adjusted through Mr. Chalker's not wholly disinterested aid.

Then the singer appeared again attired in a new and startling dress, and Joe began once more to applaud again with voice and stick. Mr. Chalker, surprised at this newly-developed enthusiasm for art, left him and walked up the hall, and sat down beside the chairman, whom he seemed to know. In fact, the chairman was also the proprietor of the show, and Mr. Chalker was acting for him in his professional capacity, much as he had acted for Mr. Emblem.

"Who is your new singer?" he asked.

"She calls herself Miss Carlotta Claradine. She's a woman, let me tell you, Mr. Chalker, who will get along. Fine figure, plenty of cheek, loud voice, flings herself about, and don't mind a bit when the words are a leetle strong. That's the kind of singer the people like. That's her husband, at the far end of the room—the big, good-looking chap with the light mustache and the cigarette in his mouth."

"Whew!" Mr. Chalker whistled the low note which indicates Surprise. "That's her husband, is it? The husband of Miss Carlotta Claradine, is it? Oho! oho! Her husband! Are you sure he is her husband?"

"Do you know him, then?"

"Yes, I know him. What was the real name of the girl?"

"Charlotte Smithers. This is her first appearance on any stage—and we made up the name for her when we first put her on the posters. I made it myself—out of Chlorodyne, you know, which is in the advertisements. Sounds well, don't it? Carlotta Claradine."

"Very well, indeed. By Jove! Her husband, is he?"

"And, I suppose," said the chairman, "lives on his wife's salary. Bless you, Mr. Chalker, there's a whole gang about every theater and music hall trying to get hold of the promising girls. It's a regular profession. Them as have nothing but their good looks may do for the mashers, but these chaps look out for the girls who'll bring in the money. What's a pretty face to them compared with the handling of a big salary every week? That's the sort Carlotta's husband belongs to."

"Well, the life will suit him down to the ground."

"And jealous with it, if you please. He comes here every night to applaud and takes her home himself. Keeps himself sober on purpose."

And then the lady appeared again in a wonderful costume of blue silk and tights, personating the Lion Masher. It was her third and last song.

In the applause which followed, Mr. Chalker could discern plainly the stick as well as the voice of his old friend. And he thought how beautiful is the love of husband unto wife, and he smiled, thinking that when Joe came next to see him, he might, perhaps, hear truths which he had thought unknown, and, for certain reasons, wished to remain unknown.

Presently he saw the singer pass down the hall, and join her husband, who now, his labors ended, was seeking refreshment at the bar. She was a good-looking girl—still only a girl, and apparently under twenty—quietly dressed, yet looking anything but quiet. But that might have been due to her fringe, which was, so to speak, a prominent-feature in her face. She was tall and well-made, with large features, an ample cheek, a full eye, and a wide mouth. A good-natured-looking girl, and though her mouth was wide, it suggested smiles. The husband was exchanging a little graceful badinage with the barmaid when she joined him, and perhaps this made her look a little cross. "She's jealous, too," said Mr. Chalker, observant; "all the better." Yet a face which, on the whole, was prepossessing and good natured, and betokened a disposition to make the best of the world.

"How long has she been married?" Mr. Chalker asked the proprietor.

"Only about a month or so."

"Ah!"

Mr. Chalker proceeded to talk business, and gave no further hint of any interest in the newly-married pair.

"Now, Joe," said the singer, with a freezing glance at the barmaid, "are you going to stand here all night?"

Joe drank off his glass and followed his wife into the street. They walked side by side in silence, until they reached their lodgings. Then she threw off her hat and jacket, and sat down on the horsehair sofa and said abruptly:

"I can't do it, Joe; and I won't. So don't ask me."

"Wait a bit—wait a bit, Lotty, my love. Don't be in a hurry, now. Don't say rash things, there's a good girl." Joe spoke quite softly, as if he were not the least angry, but, perhaps, a little hurt. "There's not a bit of a hurry. You needn't decide to-day, nor yet to-morrow."

"I couldn't do it," she said. "Oh, it's a dreadful, wicked thing even to ask me. And only five weeks to-morrow since we married!"

"Lotty, my dear, let us be reasonable." He still spoke quite softly. "If we are not to go on like other people; if we are to be continually bothering our heads about honesty, and that rubbish, we shall be always down in the world. How do other people make money and get on? By humbug, my dear. By humbug. As for you, a little play-acting is nothing."

"But I am not the man's daughter, and my own father's alive and well."

"Look here, Lotty. You are always grumbling about the music-halls."

"Well, and good reason to grumble. If you heard those ballet girls talk, and see how they go on at the back, you'd grumble. As for the music—" She laughed, as if against her will. "If anybody had told me six months ago—me, that used to go to the Cathedral Service every afternoon—that I should be a Lion Masher at a music-hall and go on dressed in tights, I should have boxed his ears for impudence."

"Why, you don't mean to tell me, Lotty, that you wish you had stuck to the moldy old place, and gone on selling music over the counter?"

"Well, then, perhaps I do."

"No, no, Lotty; your husband cannot let you say that."

"My husband can laugh and talk with barmaids. That makes him happy."

"Lotty," he said, "you are a little fool. And think of the glory. Posters with your name in letters a foot and a half long—'The People's Favorite.' Why, don't they applaud you till their hands drop off?"

She melted a little.

"Applaud! As if that did any good! And me in tights!"

"As for the tights," Joe replied with dignity, "the only person whom you need consult on that subject is your husband; and since I do not object, I should like to see the man who does. Show me that man, Lotty, and I'll straighten him out for you. You have my perfect approval, my dear. I honor you for the tights."

"My husband's approval!"

She repeated his words again in a manner which had been on other occasions most irritating to him. But to-night he refused to be offended.

"Of course," he went on, "as soon as I get a berth on another ship I shall take you off the boards. It is the husband's greatest delight, especially if he is a jolly sailor, to brave all dangers for his wife. Think, Lotty, how pleasant it would be not to do any more work."

"I should like to sing sometimes, to sing good music, at the great concerts. That's what I thought I was going to do."

"You shall; you shall sing as little or as often as you like. 'A sailor's wife a sailor's star should be.' You shall be a great lady, Lotty, and you shall just command your own line. Wait a bit, and you shall have your own carriage, and your own beautiful house, and go to as many balls as you like among the countesses and the swells."

"Oh, Joe!" she laughed. "Why, if we were as rich as anything, I should never get ladies to call upon me. And as for you, no one would ever take you to be a gentleman, you know."

"Why, what do you call me, now?"

He laughed, but without much enjoyment. No one likes to be told that he is not a gentleman, whatever his own suspicions on the subject may be.

"Never mind. I know a gentleman when I see one. Go on with your nonsense about being rich."

"I shall make you rich, Lotty, whether you like it or not," he said, still with unwonted sweetness.

She shook her head.

"Not by wickedness," she said stoutly.

"I've got there," he pulled a bundle of papers out of his pockets, "all the documents wanted to complete the case. All I want now is for the rightful heiress to step forward."

"I'm not the rightful heiress, and I'm not the woman to step forward, Joe; so don't you think it."

"I've been to-day," Joe continued, "to Doctors' Commons, and I've seen the will. There's no manner of doubt about it; and the money—oh, Lord, Lotty, if you only knew how much it is!"

"What does it matter, Joe, how much it is, if it is neither yours nor mine?"

"It matters this: that it ought all to be mine."

"How can that be, if it was not left to you?"

Joe was nothing if not a man of resource. He therefore replied without hesitation or confusion:

"The money was left to a certain man and to his heirs. That man is dead. His heiress should have succeeded, but she was kept out of her rights. She is dead, and I am her cousin, and entitled to all her property, because she made no will."

"Is that gospel truth, Joe? Is she dead? Are you sure?"

"Quite sure," he replied. "Dead as a door-nail."

"Is that the way you got the papers?"

"That's the way, Lotty."

"Then why not go to a lawyer and make him take up the case for you, and honestly get your own?"

"You don't know law, my dear, or you wouldn't talk nonsense about lawyers. There are two ways. One is to go myself to the present unlawful possessor and claim the whole. It's a woman; she would be certain to refuse, and then we should go to law, and very likely lose it all, although the right is on our side. The other way is for some one—say you—to go to her and say: 'I am that man's daughter. Here are my proofs. Here are all his papers. Give me back my own.' That you could do in the interests of justice, though I own it is not the exact truth."

"And if she refuses then?"

"She can't refuse, with the man's daughter actually standing before her. She might make a fuss for a bit. But she would have to give in at last."

"Joe, consider. You have got some papers, whatever they may contain. Suppose that it is all true that you have told me—"

"Lotty, my dear, when did I ever tell you an untruth?"

"When did you ever tell me the truth, my dear? Don't talk wild. Suppose it is all true, how are you going to make out where your heiress has been all this time, and what she has been doing?"

"Trust me for that."

"I trust you for making up something or other, but—oh, Joe, you little think, you clever people, how seldom you succeed in deceiving any one."

"I've got such a story for you, Lotty, as would deceive anybody. Listen now. It's part truth, and part—the other thing. Your father—"

"My father, poor dear man," Lotty interrupted, "is minding his music-shop in Gloucester, and little thinking what wickedness his daughter is being asked to do."

"Hang it! the girl's father, then. He died in America, where he went under another name, and you were picked up by strangers and reared under that name, in complete ignorance of your own family. All which is true and can be proved."

"Who brought her up?"

"People in America. I'm one of 'em."

"Who is to prove that?"

"I am. I am come to England on purpose. I am her guardian."

"Who is to prove that you are the girl's guardian?"

"I shall find somebody to prove that."

His thoughts turned to Mr. Chalker, a gentleman whom he judged capable of proving anything he was paid for.

"And suppose they ask me questions?"

"Don't answer 'em. You know very little. The papers were only found the other day. You are not expected to know anything."

"Where was the real girl?"

"With her grandfather."

"Where was the grandfather?"

"What does that matter?" he replied; "I will tell you afterward."

"When did the real girl die?"

"That, too, I will tell you afterward."

Lotty leaned her cheek upon her hand, and looked at her husband thoughtfully.

"Let us be plain, Joe."

"You can never be plain, my dear," he replied with the smile of a lover, not a husband; "never in your husband's eyes; not even in tights."

But she was not to be won by flattery.

"Fine words," she said, "fine words. What do they amount to? Oh, Joe, little I thought when you came along with your beautiful promises, what sort of a man I was going to marry."

"A very good sort of a man," he said. "You've got a jolly sailor—an officer and a gentleman. Come now, what have you got to say to this? Can't you be satisfied with an officer and a gentleman?"

He drew himself up to his full height. Well, he was a handsome fellow: there was no denying it.

"Good looks and fine words," his wife went on. "Well, and now I've got to keep you, and if you could make me sing in a dozen halls every night, you would, and spend the money on yourself—joyfully you would."

"We would spend it together, my dear. Don't turn rusty, Lotty."

He was not a bad-tempered man, and this kind of talk did not anger him at all. So long as his wife worked hard and brought in the coin for him to spend, what mattered for a few words now and then? Besides, he wanted her assistance.

"What are you driving at?" he went on. "I show you a bit of my hand, and you begin talking round and round. Look here, Lotty. Here's a splendid chance for us. I must have a woman's help. I would rather have your help than any other woman's— yes, than any other woman's in the world. I would indeed. If you won't help me, why, then, of course, I must go to some other woman."

His wife gasped and choked. She knew already, after only five weeks' experience, how bad a man he was—how unscrupulous, false, and treacherous, how lazy and selfish. But, after a fashion, she loved him; after a woman's fashion, she was madly jealous of him. Another woman! And only the other night she had seen him giving brandy-and-soda to one of the music-hall ballet-girls. Another woman!

"If you do, Joe," she said; "oh, if you do—I will kill her and you too!"

He laughed.

"If I do, my dear, you don't think I shall be such a fool as to tell you who she is. Do you suppose that no woman has ever fallen in love with me before you? But then, my pretty, you see I don't talk about them; and do you suppose—oh, Lotty, are you such a fool as to suppose that you are the first girl I ever fell in love with?"

"What do you want me to do? Tell me again."

"I have told you already. I want you to become, for the time, the daughter of the man who died in America; you will claim your inheritance; I will provide you with all the papers; I will stand by you; I will back you up with such a story as will disarm all suspicion. That is all."

"Yes. I understand. Haven't people been sent to prison for less, Joe?"

"Foolish people have. Not people who are well advised and under good management. Mind you, this business is under my direction. I am boss."

She made no reply, but took her candle and went off to bed.

In the dead of night she awakened her husband.

"Joe," she said, "is it true that you know another girl who would do this for you?"

"More than one, Lotty," he replied, this man of resource, although he was only half awake. "More than one. A great many more. Half-a-dozen, I know, at least."

She was silent. Half an hour afterward she woke him up again.

"Joe," she said, "I've made up my mind. You sha'n't say that I refused to do for you what any other girl in the world would have done."

As a tempter it will be seen that Joe was unsurpassed.

It was now a week since he had received, carefully wrapped in wool, and deposited in a wooden box dispatched by post, a key, newly made. It was, also, very nearly a week since he had used that key. It was used during Mr. Emblem's hour for tea, while James waited and watched outside in an agony of terror. But Joe did not find what he wanted. There were in the safe one or two ledgers, a banker's book, a check-book, and a small quantity of money. But there were not any records at all of monies invested. There were no railway certificates, waterwork shares, transfers, or notes of stock, mortgages, loans, or anything at all. The only thing that he saw was a roll of papers tied up with red tape. On the roll was written: "For Iris. To be given to her on her twenty-first birthday."

"What the deuce is this, I wonder?" Joe took this out and looked at it suspiciously. "Can he be going to give her all his money before he dies? Is he going to make her inherit it at once?" The thought was so exasperating that he slipped the roll into his pocket. "At all events," he said, "she sha'n't have them until I have read them first. I dare say they won't be missed for a day or two."

He calculated that he could read and master the contents that night, and put back the papers in the safe in the morning while James was opening the shop.

"There's nothing, James," he whispered as he went out, the safe being locked again. "There is nothing at all. Look here, my lad, you must try another way of finding out where the money is."

"I wish I was sure that he hasn't carried off something in his pocket," James murmured.

Joe spent the whole evening alone, contrary to his usual practice, which was, as we have seen, to spend it at a certain music-hall. He read the papers over and over again.

"I wish," he said at length, "I wish I had known this only two months ago. I wish I had paid more attention to Iris. What a dreadful thing it is to have a grandfather who keeps secrets from his grandson. What a game we might have had over this job! What a game we might have still if—"

And here he stopped, for the first germ or conception of a magnificent coup dawned upon him, and fairly dazzled him so that his eyes saw a bright light and nothing else.

"If Lotty would," he said. "But I am afraid she won't hear of it." He sprung to his feet and caught sight of his own face in the looking glass over the fireplace. He smiled. "I will try," he said, "I think I know by this time, how to get round most of 'em. Once they get to feel there are other women in the world besides themselves, they're pretty easy worked. I will try."

One has only to add to the revelations already made that Joe paid a second visit to the shop, this time early in the morning. The shutters were only just taken down. James was going about with that remarkable watering-pot only used in shops, which has a little stream running out of it, and Mr. Emblem was upstairs slowly shaving and dressing in his bedroom. He walked in, nodded to his friend the assistant, opened the safe, and put back the roll.

"Now," he murmured, "if the old man has really been such a dunder-headed pump as not to open the packet all these years, what the devil can he know? The name is different; he hasn't got any clew to the will; he hasn't got the certificate of his daughter's marriage, or of the child's baptism—both in the real name. He hasn't got anything. As for the girl here, Iris, having the same christian-name, that's nothing. I suppose there is more than one woman with such a fool of a name as that about in the world.

"Foxy," he said cheerfully, "have you found anything yet about the investments? Odd, isn't it? Nothing in the safe at all. You can have your key back."

He tossed him the key carelessly and went away.

The question of his grandfather's savings was grown insignificant beside this great and splendid prize which lay waiting for him. What could the savings be? At best a few thousands; the slowly saved thrift of fifty years; nobody knew better than Joe himself how much his own profligacies had cost his grandfather; a few thousands, and those settled on his Cousin Iris, so that, to get his share, he would have to try every kind of persuasion unless he could get up a case for law. But the other thing—why, it was nearly all personal estate, so far as he could learn by the will, and he had read it over and over again in the room at Somerset House, with the long table in it, and the watchful man who won't let anybody copy anything. What a shame, he thought, not to let wills be copied! Personalty sworn under a hundred and twenty thousand, all in three per cents, and devised to a certain young lady, the testator's ward, in trust, for the testator's son, or his heirs, when he or they should present themselves. Meantime, the ward was to receive for her own use and benefit, year by year, the whole income.

"It is unfortunate," said Joe, "that we can't come down upon her for arrears. Still, there's an income, a steady income, of three thousand six hundred a year when the son's heirs present themselves. I should like to call myself a solicitor, but that kite won't fly, I'm afraid. Lotty must be the sole heiress. Dressed quiet, without any powder, and her fringe brushed flat, she'd pass for a lady anywhere. Perhaps it's lucky, after all, that I married her, though if I had had the good sense to make up to Iris, who's a deuced sight prettier, she'd have kept me going almost as well with her pupils, and set me right with the old man and handed me over this magnificent haul for a finish. If only the old man hasn't broken the seals and read the papers!"

The old man had not, and Joe's fears were, therefore, groundless.

CHAPTER V

AS A BROTHER

Arnold immediately began to use the privilege accorded to him with a large and liberal interpretation. If, he argued, a man is to be treated as a brother, there should be the immediate concession of the exchange of christian-names, and he should be allowed to call as often as he pleases. Naturally he began by trying to read the secret of a life self-contained, so dull, and yet so happy, so strange to his experience.

"Is this, Iris?" he asked, "all your life? Is there nothing more?"

"No," she said; "I think you have seen all. In the morning I have my correspondence; in the afternoon I do my sewing, I play a little, I read, or I walk, sometimes by myself, and sometimes with Lala Roy; in the evening I play again, or I read again, or I work at the mathematics, while my grandfather and Lala Roy have their chess. We used to go to the theater sometimes, but of late my grandfather has not gone. At ten we go to bed. That is all my life."

"But, Iris, have you no friends at all, and no relations? Are there no girls of your own age who come to see you?"

"No, not one; I have a cousin, but he is not a good man at all. His father and mother are in Australia. When he comes here, which is very seldom, my grandfather falls ill only with thinking about him and looking at him. But I have no other relations, because, you see, I do not know who my father's people were."

"Then," said Arnold, "you may be countess in your own right; you may have any number of rich people and nice people for your cousins. Do you not sometimes think of that?"

"No" said Iris; "I never think about things impossible."

"If I were you, I should go about the streets, and walk round the picture-galleries looking for a face like your own. There cannot be many. Let me draw your face, Iris, and then we will send it to the Grosvenor, and label it, 'Wanted, this young lady's cousins.' You must have cousins, if you could only find them out."

"I suppose I must. But what if they should turn out to be rough and disagreeable people?"

"Your cousins could not be disagreeable, Iris," said Arnold.

She shook her head.

"One thing I should like," she replied. "It would be to find that my cousins, if I have any, are clever people—astronomers, mathematicians, great philosophers, and writers. But what nonsense it is even to talk of such things; I am quite alone, except for my grandfather and Lala Roy."

"And they are old," murmured Arnold.

"Do not look at me with such pity," said the girl. "I am very happy. I have my own occupation; I am independent; I have my work to fill my mind; and I have these two old gentlemen to care for and think of. They have taken so much care of me that I ought to think of nothing else but their comfort; and then there are the books down-stairs—thousands of beautiful old books always within my reach."

"But you must have some companions, if only to talk and walk with."

"Why, the books are my companions; and then Lala Roy goes for walks with me; and as for talking, I think it is much more pleasant to think."

"Where do you walk?"

"There is Battersea Park; there are the squares; and if you take an omnibus, there are the Gardens and Hyde Park."

"But never alone, Iris?"

"Oh, yes, I am often alone. Why not?"

"I suppose," said Arnold, shirking the question, because this is a civilized country, and in fact, why not? "I suppose that it is your work which keeps you from feeling life dull and monotonous."

"No life," she said, looking as wise as Newton, if Newton was ever young and handsome—"no life can be dull when one is thinking about mathematics all day. Do you study mathematics?"

"No; I was at Oxford, you know."

"Then perhaps you prefer metaphysics? Though Lala Roy says that the true metaphysics, which he has tried to teach me, can only be reached by the Hindoo intellect."

"No, indeed; I have never read any metaphysics whatever. I have only got the English intellect." This he said with intent satirical, but Iris failed to understand it so, and thought it was meant for a commendable humility.

"Physical science, perhaps?"

"No, Iris. Philosophy, mathematics, physics, metaphysics, or science of any kind have I never learned, except only the science of Heraldry, which you have taught me, with a few other things."

"Oh!" She wondered how a man could exist at all without learning these things. "Not any science at all? How can any one live without some science?"

"I knew very well," he said, "that as soon as I was found out I should be despised."

"Oh, no, not despised. But it seems such a pity—"

"There is another kind of life, Iris, which you do not know. You must let me teach you. It is the life of Art. If you would only condescend to show the least curiosity about me, Iris, I would try to show you something of the Art life."

"How can I show curiosity about you, Arnold? I feel none."

"No; that is just the thing which shames me. I have felt the most lively curiosity about you, and I have asked you thousands of impertinent questions."

"Not impertinent, Arnold. If you want to ask any more, pray do. I dare say you cannot understand my simple life."

"And you ask me nothing at all about myself. It isn't fair, Iris."

"Why should I? I know you already."

"You know nothing at all about me."

"Oh, yes, I know you very well indeed. I knew you before you came here. You showed me yourself in your letters. You are exactly like the portrait I drew of you. I never thought, for instance, that you were an old gentleman, as you thought me." He laughed. It was a new thing to see Iris using, even gently, the dainty weapons of satire.

"But you do not know what I am, or what is my profession, or anything at all about me."

"No; I do not care to know. All that is not part of yourself. It is outside you."

"And because you thought you knew me from those letters, you suffer me to come here and be your disciple still? Yet you gave me back my letters?"

"That was because they were written to me under a wrong impression."

"Will you have them back again?"

She shook her head.

"I know them all by heart," she said simply.

There was not the slightest sign of coquetry or flattery in her voice, or in her eyes, which met his look with clear and steady gaze.

"I cannot ask you to read my portrait to me as you drew it from those pictures."

"Why not?" She began to read him his portrait as readily as if she were stating the conclusion of a problem. "I saw that you were young and full of generous thoughts; sometimes you were indignant with things as they are, but generally you laughed at them and accepted them. It is, it seems, the nature of your friends to laugh a great deal at things which they ought to remedy if they could; not laugh at them. I thought that you wanted some strong stimulus to work; anybody could see that you were a man of kindly nature and good-breeding. You were careful not to offend by anything that you wrote, and I was certain that you were a man of honor. I trusted you, Arnold, before I saw your face, because I knew your soul."

"Trust me still, Iris," he said in rather a husky voice.

"Of course I did not know, and never thought, what sort of a man you were to look at. Yet I ought to have known that you were handsome. I should have guessed that from the very tone of your letters. A hunchback or a cripple could not have written in so light-hearted a strain, and I should have discovered, if I had thought of such a thing, that you were very well satisfied with your personal appearance. Young men should always be that, at least, if only to give them confidence."

"Oh, Iris—oh! Do you really think me conceited?"

"I did not say that. I only said that you were satisfied with yourself. That, I understand now, was clear, from many little natural touches in your letters."

"What else did you learn?"

"Oh, a great deal—much more than I can tell you. I knew that you go into society, and I learned from you what society means; and though you tried to be sarcastic, I understood easily that you liked social pleasure."

"Was I sarcastic?"

"Was it not sarcastic to tell me how the fine ladies, who affect so much enthusiasm for art, go to see the galleries on the private-view day, and are never seen in them again? Was it not sarcastic—"

"Spare me, Iris. I will never do it again. And knowing so much, do you not desire to know more?"

"No, Arnold. I am not interested in anything else."

"But my position, my profession, my people—are you not curious to know them?"

"No. They are not you. They are accidents of yourself."

"Philosopher! But you must know more about me. I told you I was an artist. But you have never inquired whether I was a great artist or a little one."

"You are still a little artist," she said. "I know that, without being told. But perhaps you may become great when you learn to work seriously."

"I have been lazy," he replied with something like a blush, "but that is all over now. I am going to work. I will give up society. I will take my profession seriously, if only you will encourage me."

Did he mean what he said? When he came away he used at this period to ask himself that question, and was astonished at the length he had gone. With any other girl in the world, he would have been taken at his word, and either encouraged to go on, or snubbed on the spot. But Iris received these advances as if they were a confession of weakness.

"Why do you want me to encourage you?" she asked. "I know nothing about Art. Can't you encourage yourself, Arnold?"

"Iris, I must tell you something more about myself. Will you listen for a moment? Well, I am the son of a clergyman who now holds a colonial appointment. I have got the usual number of brothers and sisters, who are doing the usual things. I will not bore you with details about them."

"No," said Iris, "please do not."

"I am the adopted son, or ward, or whatever you please, of a certain cousin. She is a single lady with a great income, which she promises to bequeath to me in the future. In the meantime, I am to have whatever I want. Do you understand the position, Iris?"

"Yes, I think so. It is interesting, because it shows why you will never be a great artist. But it is very sad."

"A man may rise above his conditions, Iris," said Arnold meekly.

"No," she went on; "it is only the poor men who do anything good. Lala Roy says so."

"I will pretend to be poor—indeed, I am poor. I have nothing. If it were not for my cousin, I could not even profess to follow Art."

"What a pity," she said, "that you are rich! Lala Roy was rich once."

Arnold repressed an inclination to desire that Lala Roy might be kept out of the conversation.

"But he gave up all his wealth and has been happy, and a philosopher, ever since."

"I can't give up my wealth, Iris, because I haven't got any—I owe my cousin everything. But for her, I should never even have known you."

He watched her at her work in the morning when she sat patiently answering questions, working out problems, and making papers. She showed him the letters of her pupils, exacting, excusing, petulant—sometimes dissatisfied and even ill-tempered, he watched her in the afternoon while she sewed or read. In the evening he sat with her while the two old men played their game of chess. Regularly every evening at half-past nine the Bengalee checkmated Mr. Emblem. Up to that hour he amused himself with his opponent, formed ingenious combinations, watched openings, and gradually cleared the board until he found himself as the hour of half-past nine drew near, able to propose a simple problem to his own mind, such as, "White moves first, to mate in three, four, or five moves," and then he proceeded to solve that problem, and checkmated his adversary.

No one, not even Iris, knew how Lala Roy lived, or what he did in the daytime. It was rumored that he had been seen at Simpson's in the Strand, but this report wanted confirmation. He had lived in Mr. Emblem's second floor for twenty years; he always paid his bills with regularity, and his long spare figure and white mustache and fez were as well known in Chelsea as any red-coated lounger among the old veterans of the Hospital.

"It is quiet for you in the evenings," said Arnold.

"I play to them sometimes. They like to hear me play during the game. Look at them."

She sat down and played. She had a delicate touch, and played soft music, such as soothes, not excites the soul. Arnold watched her, not the old men. How was it that refinement, grave, self-possession, manners, and the culture of a lady, could be found in one who knew no ladies? But then Arnold did not know Lala Roy, nor did he understand the old bookseller.

"You are always wondering about me," she said, talking while she played; "I see it in your eyes. Can you not take me as I am, without thinking why I am different from other girls? Of course I am different, because I know none of them."

"I wish they were all like you," he said.

"No; that would be a great pity. You want girls who under-stand your own life, and can enter into your pursuits—you want companions who can talk to you; go back to them, Arnold, as soon as you are tired of coming here."

And yet his instinct was right which told him that the girl was not a coquette. She had no thought—not the least thought—as yet that anything was possible beyond the existing friendship. It was pleasant, but Arnold would get tired of her, and go back to his own people. Then he would remain in her memory as a study of character. This she did not exactly formulate, but she had that feeling. Every woman makes a study of character about every man in whom she becomes ever so little interested. But we must not get conceited, my brothers, over this fact. The converse, unhappily, does not hold true. Very few men ever study the character of a woman at all. Either they fall in love with her before they have had time to make more than a sketch, and do not afterward pursue the subject, or they do not fall in love with her at all; and in the latter case it hardly seems worth while to follow up a first rough draft.

"Checkmate," said Lala Roy.

The game was finished and the evening over. "Would you like," he said, another evening, "to see my studio, or do you consider my studio outside myself?"

"I should very much like to see an artist's studio," she replied with her usual frankness, leaving it an open question whether she would not be equally pleased to see any other studio.

She came, however, accompanied by Lala Roy, who had never been in a studio before, and indeed had never looked at a picture, except with the contemptuous glance which the philosopher bestows upon the follies of mankind. Yet he came, because Iris asked him. Arnold's studio is one of the smallest of those in Tite Street. Of course it is built of red brick, and of course it has a noble staircase and a beautiful painting-room or studio proper all set about with bits of tapestry, armor, pictures, and china, besides the tools and properties of the craft. He had portfolios full of sketches; against the wall stood pictures, finished and unfinished; on an easel was a half-painted picture representing a group taken from a modern novel. Most painters only draw scenes from two novels—the "Vicar of Wakefield" and "Don Quixote;" but Arnold knew more. The central figure was a girl, quite unfinished—in fact, barely sketched in.

Iris looked at everything with the interest which belongs to the new and unexpected.

Arnold began to show the pictures in the portfolios. There were sketches of peasant life in Norway and on the Continent; there were landscapes, quaint old houses, and castles; there were ships and ports; and there were heads—hundreds of heads.

"I said you might be a great artist," said Iris. "I am sure now that you will be if you choose."

"Thank you, Iris. It is the greatest compliment you could pay me."

"And what is this?" she was before the easel on which stood the unfinished picture.

"It is a scene from a novel. But I cannot get the principal face. None of the models are half good enough. I want a sweet face, a serious face, a face with deep, beautiful eyes. Iris"—it was a sudden impulse, an inspiration—"let me put your face there. Give me my first commission."

She blushed deeply. All these drawings, the multitudinous faces and heads and figures in the portfolio were a revelation to her. And just at the very moment when she discovered that Arnold was one of those who worship beauty—a thing she had never before understood—he told her that her face was so beautiful that he must put in his picture.

"Oh, Arnold," she said, "my face would be out of place in that picture."

"Would it? Please sit down, and let me make a sketch."

He seized his crayons and began rapidly.

"What do you say, Lala Roy?" he asked by way of diversion.

"The gifts of the understanding," said the Sage, "are the treasures of the Lord; and He appointeth to every one his portion."

"Thank you," replied Arnold. "Very true and very apt, I'm sure. Iris, please, your face turned just a little. So. Ah, if I can but do some measure of justice to your eyes!"

When Iris went away, there was for the first time the least touch of restraint or self-consciousness in her. Arnold felt it. She showed it in her eyes and in the touch of her fingers when he took her hand at parting. It was then for the first time also that Arnold discovered a truth of overwhelming importance. Every new fact—everything which cannot be disputed or denied, is, we all know, of the most enormous importance. He discovered no less a truth than that he was in love with Iris. So important is this truth to a young man that it reduces the countless myriads of the world to a single pair—himself and another; it converts the most arid waste of streets into an Eden; and it blinds the eyes to ambition, riches, and success. Arnold sat down and reasoned out this truth. He said coldly and "squarely:"

"This is a girl whom I have known only a fortnight or so; she lives over a second-hand bookshop; she is a teacher by profession; she knows none of the ways of society; she would doubtless be guilty of all kinds of queer things, if she were suddenly introduced to good people; probably, she would never learn our manners," with more to the same effect, which may be reasonably omitted. Then his Conscience woke up, and said quite simply: "Arnold, you are a liar." Conscience does sometimes call hard names. She is feminine, and therefore privileged to call hard names. Else we would sometimes kick

Walter Besant

and belabor Conscience. "Arnold, don't tell more lies. You have been gradually learning to know Iris, through the wisest and sweetest letters that were ever written, for a whole year. You gradually began to know her, in fact, when you first began to interlard your letters with conceited revelations about yourself. You knew her to be sympathetic, quick, and of a most kind and tender heart. You are quite sure, though you try to disguise the fact, that she is as honest as the day, and as true as steel. As for her not being a lady, you ought to be ashamed of yourself for even thinking such a thing. Has she not been tenderly brought up by two old men who are full of honor, and truth, and all the simple virtues? Does she not look, move, and speak like the most gracious lady in the land?" "Like a goddess," Arnold confessed. "As for the ways and talk of society, what are these worth? and cannot they be acquired? And what are her manners save those of the most perfect refinement and purity?" Thus far Conscience. Then Arnold, or Arnold's secret *advocatus diaboli*, began upon another and quite different line. "She must have schemed at the outset to get me into her net; she is a siren; she assumes the disguise of innocence and ignorance the better to beguile and to deceive. She has gone home to-day elated because she thinks she has landed a gentleman."

Conscience said nothing; there are some things to which Conscience has no reply in words to offer; yet Conscience pointed to the portrait of the girl, and bade the most unworthy of all lovers look upon even his own poor and meager representation of her eyes and face, and ask whether such blasphemies could ever be forgiven.

After a self abasement, which for shame's sake we must pass over, the young man felt happier.

Henry the Second felt much the same satisfaction the morning after his scourging at the hands of the monks, who were as muscular as they were vindictive.

CHAPTER VI

COUSIN CLARA

That man who spends his days in painting a girl's portrait, in talking to her, and in gazing upon the unfinished portrait when she is not with him, and occupies his thoughts during the watches of the night in thinking about her, is perilously near to taking the last and fatal step. Flight for such a man is the only thing left, and he so seldom thinks of flight until it is too late.

Arnold was at this point.

"I am possessed by this girl," he might have said had he put his thoughts into words. "I am haunted by her eyes; her voice lingers on my ears; I dream of her face, the touch of her fingers is like the touch of an electric battery." What symptoms are these, so common that one is almost ashamed to write them down, but the infallible symptoms of love? And yet he hesitated, not because he doubted himself any longer, but because he was not independent, and such an engagement might deprive him at one stroke of all that he possessed. Might? It certainly would. Yes, the new and beautiful studio, all the things in it, all his prospects for the future, would have to be given up. "She is worth more than that," said Arnold, "and I should find work somehow. But yet, to plunge her into poverty—and to make Clara the most unhappy of women!"

The reason why Clara would be made the most unhappy of

women, was that Clara was his cousin and his benefactor, to whom he owed everything. She was the kindest of patrons, and she liked nothing so much as the lavishing upon her ward everything that he could desire. But she also, unfortunately, illustrated the truth of Chaucer's teaching, in that she loved power more than anything else, and had already mapped out Arnold's life for him.

It was his custom to call upon her daily, to use her house as his own. When they were separated, they wrote to each other every day; the relations between them were of the most intimate and affectionate kind. He advised in all her affairs, while she directed his; it was understood that he was her heir, and though she was not more than five and forty or so, and had, apparently, a long life still before her, so that the succession was distant, the prospect gave him importance. She had been out of town, and perhaps the fact of a new acquaintance with so obscure a person as a simple tutor by correspondence, seemed to Arnold not worth mentioning. At all events, he had not mentioned it in his daily letters.

And now she was coming home; she was actually arrived; he would see her that evening. Her last letter was lying before him.

> "I parted from dear Stella yesterday. She goes to stay with the Essex Mainwarings for a month; after that, I hope that she will give me a long visit. I do not know where one could find a sweeter girl, or one more eminently calculated to make a man happy. Beautiful, strictly speaking, she is not, perhaps, but of excellent connections, not without a portion, young, clever, and ambitious. With such a wife, my dear Arnold, a man may aspire to anything."

"To anything!" repeated Arnold; "what is her notion of anything? She has arrived by this time." He looked at his watch and found it was past five. "I ought to have been at the station to meet her. I must go round and see her, and I must dine with her to-night." He sighed heavily. "It would be much pleasanter to spend the evening with Iris."

Then a carriage stopped at his door. It was his cousin, and the next minute he was receiving and giving the kiss of welcome. For his own part, he felt guilty, because he could put so little heart into that kiss, compared with all previous embraces. She was a stout, hearty little woman, who could never have been in the least beautiful, even when she was young. Now on the middle line, between forty and fifty, she looked as if her face had been chopped out of the marble by a rude but determined artist, one who knew what he wanted and would tolerate no conventional work. So that her face, at all events, was, if not unique, at least unlike any other face one had ever seen. Most faces, we know, can be reduced to certain general types—even Iris's face might be classified—while of yours, my brother, there are, no doubt, multitudes. Miss Holland, however, had good eyes—bright, clear gray—the eyes of a woman who knows what she wants and means to get it if she can.

"Well, my dear," she said, taking the one comfortable chair in the studio, "I am back again, and I have enjoyed my journey very much; we will have all the travels this evening. You are looking splendid, Arnold!"

"I am very well indeed. And you, Clara? But I need not ask."

"No, I am always well. I told you about dear Stella, did I not? I never had a more delightful companion."

"So glad you liked her."

"If only, Arnold, you would like her too. But I know"—for Arnold changed color—"I know one must not interfere in these matters. But surely one may go so far with a young man one loves as to say, 'Here is a girl of a million.' There is not, Arnold, I declare, her equal anywhere; a clearer head I never met, or a better educated girl, or one who knows what a man can do, and how he can be helped to do it."

"Thank you, Clara," Arnold said coldly; "I dare say I shall discover the young lady's perfections in time."

"Not, I think, without some help. She is not an ordinary girl. You must draw her out, my dear boy."

"I will," he said listlessly. "I will try to draw her out, if you like."

"We talked a great deal of you, Arnold," Clara went on. "I confided to her some of my hopes and ambitions for you; and I am free to confess to you that she has greatly modified all my plans and calculations."

"Oh!" Arnold was interested in this "But, my dear Clara, I have my profession. I must follow my profession."

"Surely—surely! Listen, Arnold, patiently. Anybody can become an artist—anybody, of course, who has the genius. And all kinds of people, gutter people, have the genius."

"The sun," said Arnold, just as if he had been Lala Roy, "shines on all alike."

"Quite so; and there is an immense enthusiasm for art everywhere; but there is no art leader. There is no one man recognized as the man most competent to speak on art of every kind. Think of that. It is Stella's idea entirely. This man, when he is found, will sway enormous authority; he will become, if he has a wife able to assist him, an immense social power."

"And you want me to become that man?"

"Yes, Arnold. I do not see why you should not become that man. Cease to think of becoming President of the Royal Academy, yet go on painting; prove your genius, so as to command respect; cultivate the art of public speaking; and look about for a wife who will be your right hand. Think of this seriously. This is only a rough sketch, we can fill in the details afterward. But think of it. Oh, my dear boy! if I were only a man, and five-and-twenty, with such a chance before me! What a glorious career is yours, if you choose! But of course you will choose. Good gracious, Arnold! who is that?"

She pointed to the canvas on the easel, where Iris's face was like the tale of Cambuscan, half told.

"It is no one you know, Clara."

"One of your models?" She rose and examined it more closely through her glasses. "The eyes are wonderful, Arnold. They are eyes I know. As if I could ever forget them! They are the same eyes, exactly the same eyes. I have never met with any like them before. They are the eyes of my poor, lost, betrayed Claude Deseret. Where did you pick up this girl, Arnold? Is she a common model?"

"Not at all. She is not a model. She is a young lady who teaches by correspondence. She is my tutor—of course I have so often talked to you about her—who taught me the science of Heraldry, and wrote me such charming letters."

"Your tutor! You said your tutor was an old gentleman."

"So I thought, Clara. But I was wrong. My tutor is a young lady, and this is her portrait, half-finished. It does not do her any kind of justice."

"A young lady!" She looked suspiciously at Arnold, whose telltale cheek flushed. "A young lady! Indeed! And you have made her acquaintance."

"As you see, Clara; and she does me the honor to let me paint her portrait."

"What is her name, Arnold?"

"She is a Miss Aglen."

"Strange. The Deserets once intermarried with the Aglens. I wonder if she is any connection. They were Warwickshire Aglens. But it is impossible—a teacher by correspondence, a mere private governess! Who are her people?"

"She lives with her grandfather. I think her father was a tutor or journalist of some kind, but he is dead; and her grandfather keeps a second-hand bookshop in the King's Road close by."

"A bookshop! But you said, Arnold, that she was a young lady."

"So she is, Clara," he replied simply.

"Arnold!" for the first time in his life Arnold saw his cousin angry with him. She was constantly being angry with other people, but never before had she been angry with him. "Arnold, spare me this nonsense. If you have been playing with this shop-girl I cannot help it, and I beg that you will tell me no more about it, and do not, to my face, speak of her as a lady."

"I have not been playing with her, I think," said Arnold gravely; "I have been very serious with her."

"Everybody nowadays is a young lady. The girl who gives you a cup of tea in a shop; the girl who dances in the ballet; the girl who makes your dresses."

"In that case, Clara, you need not mind my calling Miss Aglen a young lady."

"There is one word left, at least: women of my class are gentlewomen."

"Miss Aglen is a gentlewoman."

"Arnold, look me in the face. My dear boy, tell me, are you mad? Oh, think of my poor unhappy Claude, what he did, and what he must have suffered!"

"I know what he did. I do not know what he suffered. My case, however, is different from his. I am not engaged to any one."

"Arnold, think of the great scheme of life I have drawn out for you. My dear boy, would you throw that all away?"

She laid her hands upon his arm and looked in his eyes with a pitiful gaze. He took her hands in his.

"My dear, every man must shape his life for himself, or must live out the life shaped for him by his fate, not by his friends. What if I see a life more delightful to me than that of which you dream?"

"You talk of a delightful life, Arnold; I spoke of an honorable career."

"Mine will be a life of quiet work and love. Yours, Clara, would be of noisy and troublesome work without love."

"Without love, Arnold? You are infatuated."

She sunk into the chair and buried her face in her hands. First, it was her lover who had deserted her for the sake of a governess, the daughter of some London tradesman; and now her adopted son, almost the only creature she loved, for whom she had schemed and thought for nearly twenty years, was ready to give up everything for the sake of another governess, also connected with the lower forms of commercial interests.

"It is very hard, Arnold," she said. "No, don't try to persuade me. I am getting an old woman, and it is too late for me to learn that a gentleman can be happy unless he marries a lady. You might as well ask me to look for happiness with a grocer."

"Not quite," said Arnold.

"It is exactly the same thing. Pray, have you proposed to this—this young lady of the second-hand bookshop?"

"No, I have not."

"You are in love with her, however?"

"I am, Clara."

"And you intend to ask her—in the shop, I dare say, among the second-hand books—to become your wife?"

"That is my serious intention, Clara."

"Claude did the same thing. His father remonstrated with him in vain, he took his wife to London, where, for a time, he lived in misery and self-reproach."

"Do you know that he reproached himself?"

"I know what must have happened when he found out his mistake. Then he went to America, where he died, no doubt in despair, although his father had forgiven him."

"The cases are hardly parallel," said Arnold. "Still, will you permit me to introduce Miss Aglen to you, if she should do me the honor of accepting me? Be generous, Clara. Do not condemn the poor girl without seeing her."

"I condemn no one—I judge no one, not even you, Arnold. But I will not receive that young woman."

"Very well, Clara."

"How shall you live, Arnold?" she asked coldly.

It was the finishing stroke—the dismissal.

"I suppose we shall not marry; but, of course, I am talking

as if—"

"As if she was ready to jump into your arms. Go on."

"We shall not marry until I have made some kind of a beginning in my work. Clara, let us have no further explanation. I understand perfectly well. But, my dear Clara," he laid his arm upon her neck and kissed her, "I shall not let you quarrel with me. I owe you too much, and I love you too well. I am always your most faithful of servants."

"No; till you are married—then—Oh, Arnold! Arnold!"

A less strong-minded woman would have burst into tears. Clara did not. She got into her carriage and drove home. She spent a miserable evening and a sleepless night. But she did not cry.

CHAPTER VII

ON BATTERSEA TERRACE

If a woman were to choose any period of her life which she pleased, for indefinite prolongation, she would certainly select that period which lies between the first perception of the first symptoms—when she begins to understand that a man has begun to love her—and the day when he tells her so.

Yet women who look back to this period with so much fondness and regret forget their little tremors and misgivings—the self-distrust, the hopes and fears, the doubts and perplexities, which troubled this time. For although it is acknowledged, and has been taught by all philosophers from King Lemuel and Lao-Kiun downward, that no greater prize can be gained by any man than the love of a good woman, which is better than a Peerage—better than a Bonanza mine—better than Name and Fame, Kudos and the newspaper paragraph, and is arrived at by much less exertion, being indeed the special gift of the gods to those they love; yet all women perfectly understand the other side to this great truth—namely, that no greater happiness can fall to any woman than the love of a good man. So that, in all the multitudinous and delightful courtships which go on around us, and in our midst, there is, on both sides, both with man and with maid, among those who truly reach to the right understanding of what this great thing may mean, a continual distrust of self, with humility and anxiety. And when, as sometimes happens, a girl has been brought up in entire ignorance of love, so that the thought of it has never entered her head, the thing itself, when it falls upon her, is overwhelming, and infolds her as with a garment from head to foot, and, except to her lover, she becomes as a sealed fountain. I know not how long this season of expectation would have lasted for Iris, but for Arnold's conversation with his cousin, which persuaded him to speak and bring matters to a final issue. To this girl, living as secluded as if she was in an Oriental harem, who had never thought of love as a thing possible for herself, the consciousness that Arnold loved her was bewildering and astonishing, and she waited, knowing that sooner or later something would be said, but trembling for fear that it should be said.

After all, it was Lala Roy, and not Clara, who finally determined Arnold to wait no longer.

He came every day to the studio with Iris when she sat for her portrait. This was in the afternoon. But he now got into the habit of coming in the morning, and would sit in silence looking on. He came partly because he liked the young man, and partly because the painter's art was new to him, and it amused him to watch a man giving his whole time and intellect to the copying or faces and things on canvas. Also, he was well aware by this time that it was not to see Mr. Emblem or himself that Arnold spent every evening at the house, and he was amused to watch the progress of an English courtship. In India, we know, they manage matters differently, and so as to give the bridegroom no more trouble than is necessary. This young man, however, took, he observed, the most wonderful pains and the most extraordinary trouble to please.

"Do you know, Lala Roy," Arnold said one morning after a silence of three hours or so, "do you know that this is going to be the portrait of the most beautiful woman in the world, and the best?"

"It is well," said the Philosopher, "when a young man desires virtue as well as beauty."

"You have known her all her life. Don't trouble yourself to speak, Lala. You can nod your head if there isn't a maxim ready. You began to lodge in the house twenty years ago, and you have seen her every day since. If she is not the best, as well as the most beautiful girl in the world, you ought to know and can contradict me. But you do know it."

"Happy is the man," said the Sage, "who shall call her wife; happy the children who shall call her mother."

"I suppose, Lala," Arnold went on with an ingenuous blush, "I suppose that you have perceived that—that—in fact—I love her."

The Philosopher inclined his head.

"Do you think—you who know her so well—that she suspects or knows it?"

"The thoughts of a maiden are secret thoughts. As well may one search for the beginnings of a river as inquire into the mind of a woman. Their ways are not our ways, nor are their thoughts ours, nor have we wit to understand, nor have they tongue to utter the things they think. I know not whether she suspects."

"Yet you have had experience, Lala Roy?"

A smile stole over the Sage's features.

"In the old days when I was young, I had experience, as all men have. I have had many wives. Yet to me, as to all others, the thoughts of the harem are unknown."

"Yet, Iris—surely you know the thoughts of Iris, your pupil."

"I know only that her heart is the abode of goodness, and that she knows not any evil thought. Young man, beware. Trouble not the clear fountain."

"Heaven knows," said Arnold, "I would not—" And here he stopped.

"Youth," said the Sage presently, "is the season for love. Enjoy the present happiness. Woman is made to be loved. Receive with gratitude what Heaven gives. The present moment is your own. Defer not until the evening what you may accomplish at noon."

With these words the oracle became silent, and Arnold sat down and began to think it all over again.

An hour later he presented himself at the house in the King's Road. Iris was alone, and she was playing.

"You, Arnold? It is early for you."

"Forgive me, Iris, for breaking in on your afternoon; but I thought—it is a fine afternoon—I thought that, perhaps—You have never taken a walk with me."

She blushed, I think in sympathy with Arnold, who looked confused and stammered, and then she said she would go with him.

They left the King's Road by the Royal Avenue, where the leaves were already thin and yellow, and passed through the Hospital and its broad grounds down to the river-side; then they turned to the right, and walked along the embankment, where are the great new red houses, to Cheyne Walk, and so across the Suspension Bridge. Arnold did not speak one word the whole way. His heart was so full that he could not trust himself to speak. Who would not be four-and-twenty again, even with all the risks and dangers of life before one, the set traps, the gaping holes, and the treacherous quicksands, if it were only to feel once more the overwhelming spirit of the mysterious goddess of the golden cestus? In silence they walked side by side over the bridge. Half-way across, they stopped and looked up the river. The tide was running in with a swift current, and the broad river was nearly at the full; the strong September sun fell upon the water, which was broken into little waves under a fresh breeze meeting the current from the north-west. There were lighters and barges majestically creeping up stream, some with brown three-cornered sails set in the bows and stern, some slowly moving with the tide, their bows kept steady by long oars, and some, lashed one to the other, forming a long train, and pulled along by a noisy little tug, all paddle wheel and engine. There was a sculler vigorously practicing for his next race, and dreaming, perhaps, of sending a challenge to Hanlan; there were some boys in a rowing-boat, laughing and splashing each other; on the north bank there was the garden of the Embankment, with its young trees still green, for the summer lasted into late September this year, and, beyond, the red brick tower of the old church, with its flag post on the top. These details are never so carefully marked as when one is anxious, and fully absorbed in things of great importance. Perhaps Arnold had crossed the bridge a hundred times before, but to day, for the first time, he noticed the common things of the river. One may be an artist, and yet may miss the treasures that lie at the very feet. This is a remark which occurs to one with each new Academy Show. With every tide the boats go up and down with their brown sails, and always the tower of Chelsea Church rises above the trees, and the broad river never forgets to sparkle and to glow in the sunshine when it gets the chance. Such common things are for the most part unheeded, but, when the mind is anxious and full, they force themselves upon one. Arnold watched boats, and river, and sunshine on the sails, with a strange interest and wonder, as one sees visions in a dream. He had seen all these things before, yet now he noticed them for the first time, and all the while he was thinking what he should say to Iris, and how he should approach the subject. I know not whether Iris, like him, saw one thing and noticed another. The thoughts of a maiden, as Lala Roy said, are secret thoughts. She looked upon the river from the bridge with Arnold. When he turned, she turned with him, and neither spoke.

They left the bridge, and passed through the wooden gate at

the Battersea end of it, and across the corner where the stone columns lie, like an imitation of Tadmor in the Desert, and so to the broad terrace overlooking the river.

There is not, anywhere, a more beautiful terrace than this of Battersea Park, especially when the tide is high. Before it lies the splendid river, with the barges which Arnold had seen from the bridge. They are broad, and flat, and sometimes squat, and sometimes black with coal, and sometimes they go up and down sideways, in lubberly Dutch fashion, but they are always picturesque; and beyond the river is the Embankment, with its young trees, which will before many years be tall and stately trees; and behind the trees are the new red palaces; and above the houses, at this time of the year and day, are the flying clouds, already colored with the light of the sinking sun. Behind the terrace are the trees, and lawns of the best-kept park in London.

In the afternoon of a late September day, there are not many who walk in these gardens. Arnold and Iris had the terrace almost to themselves, save for half-a-dozen girls with children, and two or three old men making the most of the last summer they were ever likely to see, though it would have been cruel to tell them so.

"This is your favorite walk, Iris," said Arnold at last, breaking the silence.

"Yes; I come here very often. It is my garden. Sometimes in the winter, and when the east wind blows up the river, I have it all to myself."

"A quiet life, Iris," he said, "and a happy life."

"Yes; a happy life."

"Iris, will you change it for a life which will not be so quiet?" He took her hand, but she made no reply. "I must tell you, Iris, because I cannot keep it from you any longer. I love you—oh, my dear, I cannot tell you how I love you."

"Oh, Arnold!" she whispered. It had come, the thing she feared to hear!

"May I go on? I have told you now the most important thing, and the rest matters little. Oh, Iris, may I go on and tell you all?"

"Go on," she said; "tell me all."

"As for telling you everything," He said with a little laugh, "that is no new thing. I have told you all that is in my mind for a year and more. It seems natural that I should tell you this too, even if it did not concern you at all, but some other girl; though that would be impossible. I love you, Iris; I love you— I should like to say nothing more. But I must tell you as well that I am quite a poor man; I am an absolute pauper; I have nothing at all—no money, no work, nothing. My studio and all must go back to her; and yet, Iris, in spite of this, I am so selfish as to tell you that I love you. I would give you, if I could, the most delightful palace in the world, and I offer you a share in the uncertain life of an artist, who does not know whether he has any genius, or whether he is fit even to be called an artist."

She gave him her hand with the frankness which was her chief charm, and with a look in her eyes so full of trust and truth that his heart sunk within him for very fear lest he should prove unworthy of so much confidence.

"Oh, Arnold," she said, "I think that I have loved you all along, ever since you began to write to me. And yet I never thought that love would come to me."

He led her into that bosky grove set with seats convenient for lovers, which lies romantically close to the Italian Restaurant, where they sell the cocoa and the ginger beer. There was no one in the place besides themselves, and here, among the falling leaves, and in a solitude as profound as on the top of a Dartmoor tor, Arnold told the story of his love again, and with greater coherence, though even more passion.

"Oh," said Iris again, "how could you love me, Arnold—how could you love any girl so? It is a shame, Arnold; we are not worth so much. Could any woman," she thought, "be worth the wealth of passion and devotion which her lover poured out for her?"

"My tutor," he went on, "if you only knew what things you have taught me, a man of experience! If I admired you when I thought you must be a man, and pictured an old scholar full of books and wisdom, what could I do when I found that a young girl had written those letters? You gave mine back to me; did you think that I would ever part with yours? And you owned—oh, Iris, what would not the finished woman of the world give to have the secret of your power?—you owned that you knew all my letters, every one, by heart. And after all, you will love me, your disciple and pupil, and a man who has his way to make from the very beginning and first round of the ladder. Think, Iris, first. Is it right to throw away so much upon a man who is worth so little?"

"But I am glad that you are poor. If you were rich I should have been afraid—oh, not of you, Arnold—never of you, but of your people. And, besides it is so good—oh, so very good for a young man—a young man of the best kind, not my cousin's kind—to be poor. Nobody ought ever to be allowed to become rich before he is fifty years of age at the very least. Because now you will have to work in earnest, and you will become a great artist—yes, a truly great artist, and we shall be proud of you."

"You shall make of me what you please, and what you can. For your sake, Iris, I wish I were another Raphael. You are my mistress and my queen. Bid me to die, and I will dare—Iris, I swear that the words of the extravagant old song are real to me."

"Nay," she said, "not your queen, but your servant always. Surely love cannot command. But, I think," she added softly, with a tender blush; "I think—nay, I am sure and certain that it can obey."

He stooped and kissed her fingers.

"My love," he murmured; "my love—my love!"

The shadows lengthened and the evening fell; but those two foolish people sat side by side, and hand in hand, and what they said further we need not write down, because to tell too much of what young lovers whisper to each other is a kind of sacrilege.

At last Arnold became aware that the sun was actually set, and he sprung to his feet.

They walked home again across the Suspension Bridge. In the western sky was hanging a huge bank of cloud all bathed in purple, red and gold; the river was ablaze; the barges floated in a golden haze; the light shone on their faces, and made them all glorious, like the face of Moses, for they, too, had stood— nay, they were still standing—at the very gates of Heaven.

"See, Iris," said the happy lover, "the day is done; your old life is finished; it has been a happy time, and it sets in glory and splendor. The red light in the west is a happy omen of the day to come."

So he took her hand, and led her over the river, and then to his own studio in Tite Street. There, in the solemn twilight, he held her in his arms, and renewed the vows of love with kisses and fond caresses.

"Iris, my dear—my dear—you are mine and I am yours. What have I done to deserve this happy fate?"

CHAPTER VIII

THE DISCOVERY

At nine o'clock that evening, Mr. Emblem looked up from the chess board.

"Where is Mr. Arbuthnot this evening, my dear?" he asked.

It would be significant in some houses when a young man is expected every evening. Iris blushed, and said that perhaps he was not coming. But he was, and his step was on the stair as she spoke.

"You are late, Mr. Arbuthnot," said Mr. Emblem, reproachfully, "you are late, sir, and somehow we get no music now until you come. Play us something, Iris. It is my move, Lala—"

Iris opened the piano and Arnold sat down beside her, and their eyes met. There was in each the consciousness of what had passed.

"I shall speak to him to-night, Iris," Arnold whispered. "I have already written to my cousin. Do not be hurt if she does not call upon you."

"Nothing of that sort will hurt me," Iris said, being ignorant of social ways, and without the least ambition to rise in the world. "If your cousin does not call upon me I shall not be disappointed. Why should she want to know me? But I am sorry, Arnold, that she is angry with you."

Lala Roy just then found himself in presence of a most beautiful problem—white to move and checkmate in three moves. Mr. Emblem found the meshes of fate closing round him earlier than usual, and both bent their heads closely over the table.

"Checkmate!" said Lala Roy. "My friend, you have played badly this evening."

"I have played badly," Mr. Emblem replied, "because to-morrow will be an important day for Iris, and for myself. A day, Iris, that I have been looking forward to for eighteen years, ever since I got your father's last letter, written upon his death-bed. It seems a long time, but like a lifetime," said the old man of seventy-five, "it is as nothing when it is gone. Eighteen years, and you were a little thing of three, child!"

"What is going to happen to me, grandfather, except that I shall be twenty-one?"

"We shall see to-morrow. Patience, my dear—patience."

He spread out his hands and laughed. What was going to happen to himself was a small thing compared with the restoration of Iris to her own.

"Mr. Emblem," said Arnold, "I also have something of importance to say."

"You, too, Mr. Arbuthnot? Cannot yours wait also until to-morrow?"

"No; it is too important. It cannot wait an hour."

"Well, sir"—Mr. Emblem pushed up his spectacles and leaned back in his chair—"well, Mr. Arbuthnot, let us have it."

"I think you may guess what I have to say, Mr. Emblem. I am sure that Lala Roy has already guessed it."

The philosopher inclined his head in assent.

"It is that I have this afternoon asked Iris to marry me, Mr. Emblem. And she has consented."

"Have you consented, Iris, my dear?" said her grandfather.

She placed her hand in Arnold's for reply.

"Do you think you know him well enough, my dear?" Mr. Emblem asked gravely, looking at her lover. "Marriage is a serious thing: it is a partnership for life. Children, think well before you venture on the happiness or ruin of your whole lives. And you are so young. What a pity—what a thousand pities that people were not ordained to marry at seventy or so!"

"We have thought well," said Arnold. "Iris has faith in me."

"Then, young man, I have nothing to say. Iris will marry to please herself, and I pray that she may be happy. As for you, I like your face and manners, but I do not know who you are, nor what your means may be. Remember that I am poor—I am so poor—I can tell you all now, that to-morrow we shall—well, patience—to-morrow I shall most likely have my very stock seized and sold."

"Your stock sold? Oh, grandfather!" cried Iris; "and you did not tell me! And I have been so happy."

"Friend," said Lala, "was it well to hide this from me?"

"Foolish people," Mr. Emblem went on, "have spread reports that I am rich, and have saved money for Iris. It is not true, Mr. Arbuthnot. I am not rich. Iris will come to you empty-handed."

"And as for me, I have nothing," said Arnold, "except a pair of hands and all the time there is. So we have all to gain and nothing to lose."

"You have your profession," said Iris, "and I have mine. Grandfather, do not fear, even though we shall all four become poor together."

It seemed natural to include Lala Roy, who had been included with them for twenty years.

"As for Iris being empty-handed," said Arnold, "how can that ever be? Why, she carries in her hands an inexhaustible cornucopia, full of precious things."

"My dear," said the old man, holding out his arms to her, "I could not keep you always. Some day I knew you would leave me; it is well that you should leave me when I am no longer able to keep a roof over your head."

"But we shall find a roof for you, grandfather, somewhere. We shall never part."

"The best of girls always," said Mr. Emblem; "the best of girls! Mr. Arbuthnot, you are a happy man."

Then the Sage lifted up his voice and said solemnly:

"On her tongue dwelleth music; the sweetness of honey floweth from her lips; humility is like a crown of glory about her head; her eye speaketh softness and love; her husband putteth his heart in her bosom and findeth joy."

"Oh, you are all too good to me," murmured Iris.

"A friend of mine," said Mr. Emblem, "now, like nearly all my friends, beneath the sod, used to say that a good marriage was a happy blending of the finest Wallsend with the most delicate Silkstone. But he was in the coal trade. For my own part I have always thought that it is like the binding of two scarce volumes into one."

"Oh, not second-hand volumes, grandfather," said Iris.

"I don't know. Certainly not new ones. Not volumes under one-and-twenty, if you please. Mr. Arbuthnot, I am glad; you will know why very soon. I am very glad that Iris made her choice before her twenty-first birthday. Whatever may happen now, no one can say that either of you was influenced by any expectations. You both think yourself paupers; well, I say nothing, because I know nothing. But, children, if a great thing happen to you, and that before four-and-twenty hours have passed, be prepared—be prepared, I say—to receive it with moderate rejoicing."

"To-morrow?" Iris asked. "Why to-morrow? Why not to-night, if you have a secret to tell us?"

"Your father enjoined in his last letter to wait till you were twenty-one. The eve of your birthday, however, is the same thing as your birthday. We will open the papers to-night. What I have to tell you, Iris, shall be told in the presence of your lover, whatever it is—good or bad."

He led the way down-stairs into the back shop. Here he lit the gas, and began to open his case, slowly and cautiously.

"Eighteen years ago, Iris, my child, I received your father's last letter, written on his death bed. This I have already told you. He set down, in that letter, several things which surprised me very much. We shall come to these things presently. He also laid down certain instructions for your bringing up, my dear. I was, first of all, to give you as good an education as I could afford; I was to keep you as much as possible separated from companions who might not be thought afterward fit to be the friends of a young lady. You have as good an education as Lala Roy and I could devise between us. From him you have learned mathematics, so as to steady your mind and make you

Walter Besant

exact; and you have learned the science of heraldry from me, so that you may at once step into your own place in the polite world, where, no doubt, it is a familiar and a necessary study. You have also learned music, because that is an accomplishment which every one should possess. What more can any girl want for any station? My dear, I am happy to think that a gentleman is your lover. Let him tell us, now—Lala Roy and me—to our very faces, if he thinks we have, between us, made you a lady."

Arnold stooped and kissed her hand.

"There is no more perfect lady," he said, "in all the land."

"Iris's father, Mr. Arbuthnot, was a gentleman of honorable and ancient family, and I will tell you, presently, as soon as I find it out myself, his real name. As for his coat-of-arms, he bore Quarterly, first and fourth, two roses and a boar's head erect; second and third, gules and fesse between—strange, now that I have forgotten what it was between. Everybody calls himself a gentleman nowadays; even Mr. Chalker, who is going to sell me up, I suppose; but everybody, if you please, is not armiger. Iris, your father was armiger. I suppose I am a gentleman on Sundays, when I go to church with Iris, and wear a black coat. But your father, my dear, though he married my daughter, was a gentleman by birth. And one who knows heraldry respects a gentleman by birth." He laid his hand now on the handle of the safe, as if the time were nearly come for opening it, but not quite. "He sent me, with this last letter, a small parcel for you, my dear, not to be opened until you reached the age of twenty-one. As for the person who had succeeded to his inheritance, she was to be left in peaceable possession for a reason which he gave—quite a romantic story, which I will tell you presently—until you came of age. He was very urgent on this point. If, however, any disaster of sickness or misfortune fell upon me, I was to act in your interests at once, without waiting for time. Children," the old man added solemnly, "by the blessing of Heaven—I cannot take it as anything less—I have been spared in health and fortune until this day. Now let me depart in peace, for my trust is expired, and my child is safe, her inheritance secured, with a younger and better protector." He placed the key in the door of the safe. "I do not know, mind," he said, still hesitating to take the final step; "I do not know the nature of the inheritance; it may be little or maybe great. The letter does not inform me on this point. I do not even know the name of the testator, my son-in-law's father. Nor do I know the name of my daughter's husband. I do not even know your true name, Iris, my child. But it is not Aglen."

"Then, have I been going under a false name all my life?"

"It was the name your father chose to bear for reasons which seemed good and sufficient to him, and these are part of the story which I shall have to tell you. Will you have this story first, or shall we first open the safe and read the contents of the parcel?"

"First," said Arnold, "let us sit down and look in each other's faces."

It was a practical suggestion. But, as it proved, it was an unlucky one, because it deprived them of the story.

"Iris," he said, while they waited, "this is truly wonderful!"

"Oh, Arnold! What am I to do with an inheritance?"

"That depends on what it is. Perhaps it is a landed estate; in which case we shall not be much better off, and can go on with our work; perhaps there will be houses; perhaps it will be thousands of pounds, and perhaps hundreds. Shall we build a castle in the air to suit our inheritance?"

"Yes; let us pretend. Oh, grandfather, stop one moment! Our castle, Arnold, shall be, first of all, the most beautiful studio in the world for you. You shall have tapestry, blue china, armor, lovely glass, soft carpets, carved doors and painted panels, a tall mantelshelf, old wooden cabinets, silver cups, and everything else what one ought to like, and you shall choose everything for yourself, and never get tired of it. But you must go on painting; you must never stop working, because we must be proud of you as well that you like. Oh, but I have not done yet. My grandfather is to have two rooms for himself, which he can fill with the books he will spend his time in collecting; Lala Roy will have two more rooms, quite separate, where he can sit by himself whenever he does not choose to sit with me; I shall have my own study to myself, where I shall go on reading mathematics; and we shall all have, between us, the most beautiful dining-room and drawing-room that you ever saw; and a garden and a fountain, and—yes—money to give to people who are not so fortunate as ourselves. Will that do, Arnold?"

"Yes, but you have almost forgotten yourself, dear. There must be carriages for you, and jewels, and dainty things all your own, and a boudoir, and nobody shall think of doing or saying anything in the house at all, except for your pleasure; will that do, Iris?"

"I suppose we shall have to give parties of some kind, and to go to them. Perhaps one may get to like society. You will teach me lawn-tennis, Arnold; and I should like, I think, to learn dancing. I suppose I must leave off making my own dresses, though I know that I shall never be so well dressed if I do. And about the cakes and puddings—but, oh, there is enough pretending."

"It is difficult," said Lala Roy, "to bear adversity. But to be temperate in prosperity is the height of wisdom."

"And now suppose, Iris," said Arnold "that the inheritance, instead of being thousands a year, is only a few hundreds."

"Ah, then, Arnold, it will be ever so much simpler. We shall have something to live upon until you begin to make money for us all."

"Yes; that is very simple. But suppose, again, that the inheritance is nothing but a small sum of money."

"Why, then," said Iris, "we will give it all to grandfather, who will pay off his creditor, and we will go on as if nothing had happened."

"Child!" said Mr. Emblem, "do you think that I would take your little all?"

"And suppose, again," Arnold went on, "that the inheritance turns out a delusion, and that there is nothing at all?"

"That cannot be supposed," said Mr. Emblem quickly; "that is absurd!"

"If it were," said Iris, "we shall only be, to-morrow, just exactly what we are to-day. I am a teacher by correspondence, with five pupils. Arnold is looking for art-work, which will pay; and between us, my dear grandfather and Lala Roy, we are going to see that you want nothing."

Always Lala Roy with her grandfather, as if their interests were identical, and, indeed, he had lived so long with them that Iris could not separate the two old men.

"We will all live together," Iris continued, "and when our fortune is made we will all live in a palace. And now, grandfather, that we have relieved our feelings, shall we have the story and the opening of the papers in the safe?"

"Which will you have first?" Mr. Emblem asked again.

"Oh, the safe," said Arnold. "The story can wait. Let us examine the contents of the safe."

"The story," said Mr. Emblem, "is nearly all told in your father's letter, my dear. But there is a little that I would tell you first, before I read that letter. You know, Iris, that I have never been rich; my shop has kept me up till now, but I have never been able to put by money. Well—my daughter Alice, your poor mother, my dear, who was as good and clever as you are, was determined to earn her own living, and so she went out as a governess. And one day she came home with her husband; she had been married the day before, and she told me they had very little money, and her husband was a scholar and a gentleman, and wanted to get work by writing. He got some, but not enough, and they were always in a poor way, until one day he got a letter from America—it was while the Civil War was raging—from an old Oxford friend, inviting him to emigrate and try fortune as a journalist out there. He went, and his wife was to join him. But she died, my dear; your mother died, and a year later I had your father's last letter, which I am now going to read to you."

"One moment, sir," said Arnold. "Before you open the safe and take out the papers, remember that Iris and I can take nothing—nothing at all for ourselves until all your troubles are tided over."

"Children—children," cried Mr. Emblem.

"Go, my son, to the Desert," observed the Sage, standing solemnly upright like a Prophet of Israel. "Observe the young stork of the wilderness, how he beareth on his wings his aged sire and supplieth him with food. The piety of a child is sweeter than the incense of Persia offered to the sun; yea, more delicious is it than the odors from a field of Arabian spice."

"Thank you, Lala," said Mr. Emblem. "And now, children, we will discover the mystery."

He unlocked the safe and threw it open with somewhat of a theatrical air. "The roll of papers." He took it out. "'For Iris to be opened on her twenty-first birthday.' And this is the eve of it. But where is the letter? I tied the letter round it, with a piece of tape. Very strange. I am sure I tied the letter with a piece of tape. Perhaps it was—Where is the letter?"

He peered about in the safe; there was nothing else in it except a few old account books; but he could not find the letter! Where could it be?

"I remember," he said—"most distinctly I remember tying up the letter with the parcel. Where can it be gone to?"

A feeling of trouble to come seized him. He was perfectly sure he had tied up the letter with the parcel, and here was the parcel without the letter, and no one had opened the safe except himself.

"Never mind about the letter, grandfather," said Iris; "we shall find that afterward."

"Well, then, let us open the parcel."

It was a packet about the size of a crown-octavo volume, in brown paper, carefully fastened up with gum, and on the face of it was a white label inscribed: "For Iris, to be opened on her twenty-first birthday." Everybody in turn took it, weighed it, so to speak, looked at it curiously, and read the legend. Then they returned it to Mr. Emblem, who laid it before him and produced a penknife. With this, as carefully and solemnly as if he were offering up a sacrifice or performing a religious function, he cut the parcel straight through.

"After eighteen years," he said; "after eighteen years. The ink will be faded and the papers yellow. But we shall see the certificates of the marriage and of your baptism, Iris; there will also be letters to different people, and a true account of the rupture with his father, and the cause, of which his letter spoke. And of course we shall find out what was his real name and what is the kind of inheritance which has been waiting for you so long, my dear. Now then."

The covering incase of the packet was a kind of stiff cardboard or millboard, within brown paper. Mr. Emblem laid it open. It was full of folded papers. He took up the first and opened it.

The paper was blank. The next, it was blank; the third, it was blank; the fourth, and fifth, and sixth, and so on throughout. The case, which had been waiting so long, waiting for eighteen years, to be opened on Iris's twenty-first birthday, was full of blank papers. They were all half sheets of note-paper.

Mr. Emblem looked surprised at the first two or three papers; then he turned pale; then he rushed at the rest. When he had opened all, he stared about him with bewilderment.

"Where is the letter?" he asked again. Then he began with trembling hands to tear out the contents of the safe and spread them upon the table. The letter was nowhere.

"I am certain," he said, for the tenth time, "I am quite certain that I tied up the letter with red tape, outside the packet. And no one has been at the safe except me."

"Tell us," said Arnold, "the contents of the letter as well as you remember them. Your son-in-law was known to you under the name of Aglen, which was not his real name. Did he tell you his real name?"

"No."

"What did he tell you? Do you remember the letter?"

"I remember every word of the letter."

"If you dictate it, I will write it down. That may be a help."

Mr. Emblem began quickly, and as if he was afraid of forgetting:

"When you read these lines, I shall be in the Silent Land, whither Alice, my wife, has gone before me."

Then Mr. Emblem began to stammer.

"'In one small thing we deceived you, Alice and I. My name is not Aglen'—is not Aglen—"

And here a strange thing happened. His memory failed him at this point.

"Take time," said Arnold; "there is no hurry."

Mr. Emblem shook his head.

"I shall remember the rest to-morrow, perhaps," he said.

"Is there anything else you have to help us?" asked Arnold: "never mind the letter, Mr. Emblem. No doubt that will come back presently. You see we want to find out, first, who Iris's father really was, and what is her real name. There was his coat-of-arms. That will connect her with some family, though it may be a family with many branches."

"Yes—oh yes! his coat-of-arms. I have seen his signet-ring a dozen times. Yes, his coat; yes, first and fourth, two roses and a boar's head erect; second and third—I forget."

"Humph! Was there any one who knew him before he was married?"

"Yes, yes," Mr. Emblem sat up eagerly. "Yes, there is—there is; he is my oldest customer. But I forget his name, I have forgotten everything. Perhaps I shall get back my memory to-morrow. But I am old. Perhaps it will never get back."

He leaned his head upon his hands, and stared about him with bewildered eyes.

"I do not know, young man," he said presently, addressing Arnold, "who you are. If you come from Mr. Chalker, let me tell you it is a day too soon. To-morrow we will speak of business." Then he sprung to his feet suddenly, struck with a thought which pierced him like a dagger. "To-morrow! It is the day when they will come to sell me up. Oh, Iris! what did that matter when you were safe? Now we are all paupers together—all paupers."

He fell back in his chair white and trembling. Iris soothed him; kissed his cheek and pressed his hand; but the terror and despair of bankruptcy were upon him. This is an awful specter, which is ever ready to appear before the man who has embarked his all in one venture. A disastrous season, two or three unlucky ventures, a succession of bad debts, and the grisly specter stands before them. He had no terror for the old man so long as he thought that Iris was safe. But now—

"Idle talk, Iris—idle talk, child," he said, when they tried to comfort him. "How can a girl make money by teaching? Idle talk, young man. How can money be made by painting? It's as bad a trade as writing. How can money be made anyhow but in an honest shop? And to-morrow I shall have no shop, and we shall all go into the street together!"

Presently, when lamentations had yielded to despair, they persuaded him to go to bed. It was past midnight. Iris went upstairs with him, while Lala Roy and Arnold waited down below. And then Arnold made a great discovery. He began to examine the folded papers which were in the packet. I think he had some kind of vague idea that they might contain secret and invisible writing. They were all sheets of note-paper, of the same size, folded in the same way—namely, doubled as if for a square envelope. On holding one to the light, he read the water-mark:

HIEROGLYPHICA
A Vegetable Vellum.
M.S. & Co.

They all had the same water-mark. He showed the thing to the Hindoo, who did not understand what it meant.

Then Iris came down again. Her grandfather was sleeping.

Like a child, he fell asleep the moment his head fell upon the pillow.

"Iris," he said, "this is no delusion of your grandfather's. The parcel has been robbed."

"How do you know, Arnold?"

"The stupid fellow who stole and opened the packet no doubt thought he was wonderfully clever to fill it up again with paper. But he forgot that the packet has been lying for eighteen years in the safe, and that this note-paper was made the day before yesterday."

"How do you know that?"

"You can tell by the look and feel of the paper; they did not make paper like this twenty years ago; besides, look at the water-mark;" he held it to the light, and Iris read the mystic words. "That is the fashion of to-day. One house issues a new kind of paper, with a fancy name, and another imitates them. To-morrow, I will ascertain exactly when this paper was made."

"But who would steal it, Arnold? Who could steal it?"

"It would not probably be of the least use to any one. But it might be stolen in order to sell it back. We may see an advertisement carefully worded, guarded, or perhaps—Iris, who had access to the place, when your grandfather was out?"

"No one but James, the shopman. He has been here five-and-twenty years. He would not, surely, rob his old master. No one else comes here except the customers and Cousin Joe."

"Joe is not, I believe, quite—"

"Joe is a very bad man. He has done dreadful things. But then, even if Joe were bad enough to rob the safe, how could he get

Walter Besant

at it? My grandfather never leaves it unlocked. Oh, Arnold, Arnold, that all this trouble should fall upon us on the very day—"

"My dear, is it not better that it should fall upon you when I am here, one more added to your advisers? If you have lost a fortune, I have found one. Think that you have given it to me."

"Oh, the fortune may go," she said. "The future is ours, and we are young. But who shall console my grandfather in his old age for his bankruptcy?"

"As the stream," said Lala Roy, "which passeth from the mountains to the ocean, kisseth every meadow on its way, yet tarries not in any place, so Fortune visits the sons of men; she is unstable as the wind; who shall hold her? Let not adversity tear off the wings of hope."

They could do nothing more. Arnold replaced the paper in the packet, and gave it to Iris; they put back the ledgers and account-books in the safe, and locked it up, and then they went upstairs.

"You shall go to bed, Iris," said Arnold, "and you, too, Lala Roy. I shall stay here, in case Mr. Emblem should—should want anything."

He was, in reality, afraid that "something would happen" to the old man. His sudden loss of memory, his loss of self-control when he spoke of his bankruptcy, the confusion of his words, told clearly of a mind unhinged. He could not go away and leave Iris with no better protection than one other weak old man.

He remained, but Iris sat with him, and in the silent watches of the night they talked about the future.

Under every roof are those who talk about the future, and

those who think about the past; so the shadow of death is always with us and the sunshine of life. Not without reason is the Roman Catholic altar incomplete without a bone of some dead man. As for the thing which had been stolen, that affected them but little. What does it matter—the loss of what was promised but five minutes since?

It was one o'clock in the morning when Lala Roy left them. They sat at the window, hand-in-hand, and talked. The street below them was very quiet; now and then a late cab broke the silence, or the tramp of a policeman; but there were no other sounds. They sat in darkness because they wanted no light. The hours sped too swiftly for them. At five the day began to dawn.

"Iris," said Arnold, "leave me now, and try to sleep a little. Shall we ever forget this night of sweet and tender talk?"

When she was gone, he began to be aware of footsteps overhead in the old man's room. What was he going to do? Arnold waited at the door. Presently the door opened, and he heard careful steps upon the stairs. They were the steps of Mr. Emblem himself. He was fully dressed, with his usual care and neatness, his black silk stock buckled behind, and his white hair brushed.

"Ah, Mr. Arbuthnot," he said cheerfully, "you are early this morning!" as if it was quite a usual thing for his friends to look in at six in the morning.

"You are going down to the shop, Mr. Emblem?"

"Yes, certainly—to the shop. Pray come with me."

Arnold followed him.

"I have just remembered," said the old man, "that last night we did not look on the floor. I will have one more search for the letter, and then, if I cannot find it, I will write it all out—every word. There is not much, to be sure, but the story is told without the names."

"Tell me the story, Mr. Emblem, while you remember it."

"All in good time, young man. Youth is impatient."

He drew up the blind and let in the morning light; then he began his search for the letter on the floor, going on his hands and knees, and peering under the table and chairs with a candle. At length he desisted.

"I tied it up," he said, "with the parcel, with red tape. Very well—we must do without it. Now, Mr. Arbuthnot, my plan is this. First, I will dictate the letter. This will give you the outlines of the story. Next, I will send you to—to my old customer, who can tell you my son-in-law's real name. And then I will describe his coat-of-arms. My memory was never so clear and good as I feel it to-day. Strange that last night I seemed, for the moment, to forget everything! Ha, ha! Ridiculous, wasn't it? I suppose—But there is no accounting for these queer things. Perhaps I was disappointed to find nothing in the packet. Do you think, Mr. Arbuthnot, that I—" Here he began to tremble. "Do you think that I dreamed it all? Old men think strange things. Perhaps—"

"Let us try to remember the letter, Mr. Emblem."

"Yes, yes—certainly—the letter. Why it went—ahem!—as follows—"

*　　*　　*　　*　　*

Arnold laid down the pen in despair. The poor old man was mad. He had poured out the wildest farrago without sense, coherence, or story.

"So much for the letter, Mr. Arbuthnot." He was mad without doubt, yet he knew Arnold, and knew, too, why he was in the house. "Ah, I knew it would come back to me. Strange if it did not. Why I read that letter once every quarter or so for eighteen years. It is a part of myself. I could not forget it."

"And the name of your son-in-law's old friend?"

"Oh, yes, the name!"

He gave some name, which might have been the lost name, but as Mr. Emblem changed it the next moment, and forgot it again the moment after, it was doubtful; certainly not much to build upon.

"And the coat-of-arms?"

"We are getting on famously, are we not? The coat, sir, was as follows."

He proceeded to describe an impossible coat—a coat which might have been drawn by a man absolutely ignorant of science.

All this took a couple of hours. It was now eight o'clock.

"Thank you, Mr. Emblem," said Arnold. "I have no doubt now that we shall somehow bring Iris to her own again, in spite of your loss. Shall we go upstairs and have some breakfast?"

"It is all right, Iris," cried the old man gleefully. "It is all right. I have remembered everything, and Mr. Arbuthnot will go out presently and secure your inheritance."

Iris looked at Arnold.

"Yes, dear," she said. "You shall have your breakfast. And then you shall tell me all about it when Arnold goes; and you will take a holiday, won't you—because I am twenty-one to-day?"

"Aha!" He was quite cheerful and mirthful, because he had recovered his memory. "Aha, my dear, all is well! You are twenty-one, and I am seventy-five; and Mr. Arbuthnot will go and bring home the—the inheritance. And I shall sit here all day long. It was a good dream that came to me this morning, was it not? Quite a voice from Heaven, which said: 'Get up and write down the letter while you remember it.' I got up; I found by the—by the merest accident, Mr. Arbuthnot on the stairs, and we have arranged everything for you—everything."

CHAPTER IX

DR. WASHINGTON

Arnold returned to his studio, sat down and fell fast asleep.

He was awakened about noon by his Cousin Clara.

"Oh, Arnold," she cried, shaking him wrathfully by the arm, "this is a moment of the greatest excitement and importance to me, and you are my only adviser, and you are asleep!"

He sprung to his feet.

"I am awake now, Clara. Anxiety and trouble? On account of our talk yesterday?"

He saw that she had been crying. In her hands she had a packet of letters.

"Oh, no, no; it is far more important than that. As for our talk—"

"I am engaged to her, Clara."

"So I expected," she replied coldly. "But I am not come here about your engagement. And you do not want my congratulations, I suppose?"

"I should like to have your good wishes, Clara."

Walter Besant

"Oh, Arnold, that is what my poor Claude said when he deserted me and married the governess. You men want to have your own way, and then expect us to be delighted with it."

"I expect nothing, Clara. Pray understand that."

"I told Claude, when he wrote asking forgiveness, that he had my good wishes, whatever he chose to do, but that I would not on any account receive his wife. Very well, Arnold; that is exactly what I say to you."

"Very well, Clara. I quite understand. As for the studio, and all the things that you have given me, they are, of course, yours again. Let me restore what I can to you."

"No, Arnold, they are yours. Let me hear no more about things that are your own. Of course, your business, as you call it, is exciting. But as for this other thing, it is far more important. Something has happened; something I always expected; something that I looked forward to for years; although it has waited on the way so long, it has actually come at last, when I had almost forgotten to look for it. So true it is, Arnold, that good fortune and misfortune alike come when we least expect them."

Arnold sat down. He knew his cousin too well to interrupt her. She had her own way of telling a story, and it was a roundabout way.

"I cannot complain, after twenty years, can I? I have had plenty of rope, as you would say. But still it has come at last. And naturally, when it does come, it is a shock."

"Is it hereditary gout, Clara?"

"Gout! Nonsense, Arnold! When the will was read, I said to myself, 'Claude is certain to come back and claim his own. It is his right, and I hope he will come. But for my own part, I have not the least intention of calling upon the governess.' Then three or four years passed away, and I heard—I do not remember how—that he was dead. And then I waited for his heirs, his children, or their guardians. But they did not come."

"And now they have really come? Oh, Clara, this is indeed a misfortune."

"No, Arnold; call it a restitution, not a misfortune. I have been living all these years on the money which belongs to Claude's heirs."

"There was a son, then. And now he has dropped upon us from the clouds?"

"It is a daughter, not a son. But you shall hear. I received a letter this morning from a person called Dr. Joseph Washington, stating that he wrote to me on account of the only child and heiress of the late Claude Deseret."

"Who is Dr. Joseph Washington?"

"He is a physician, he says, and an American."

"Yes; will you go on?"

"I do not mind it, Arnold; I really do not. I must give up my house and put down my carriage, but it is for Claude's daughter. I rejoice to think that he has left some one behind him. Arnold, that face upon your canvas really has got eyes wonderfully like his, if it was not a mere fancy, when I saw it yesterday. I am glad, I say, to give up everything to the child of Claude."

"You think so kindly of him, Clara, who inflicted so much pain on you."

"I can never think bitterly of Claude. We were brought up together; we were like brother and sister; he never loved me in any other way. Oh, I understood it all years ago. To begin with, I was never beautiful; and it was his father's mistake. Well: this American followed up his letter by a visit. In the letter he merely said he had come to London with the heiress. But he called an hour ago, and brought me—oh, Arnold, he brought me one more letter from Claude. It has been waiting for me for eighteen years. After all that time, after eighteen years, my poor dead Claude speaks to me again. My dear, when I thought he was miserable on account of his marriage, I was wrong. His wife made him happy, and he died because she died." The tears came into her eyes again. "Poor boy! Poor Claude! The letter speaks of his child. It says—" She opened and read the letter. "He says: 'Some day my child will, I hope, come to you, and say: Cousin Clara, I am Iris Deseret.'"

"Iris?" said Arnold.

"It is her name, Arnold. It was the child's grandmother's name."

"A strange coincidence," he said. "Pray go on."

"'She will say: Cousin Clara, I am Iris Deseret. Then you will be kind to her, as you would to me, if I were to come home again.' I cannot read any more, my dear, even to you."

"Did this American give you any other proof of what he asserts?"

"He gave me a portrait of Claude, taken years ago, when he was a boy of sixteen, and showed me the certificate of marriage, and the child's certificate of baptism, and letters from his wife. I suppose nothing more can be wanted."

"I dare say it is all right, Clara. But why was not the child brought over before?"

"Because—this is the really romantic part of the story—when her father died, leaving the child, she was adopted by these charitable Americans, and no one ever thought of examining the papers, which were lying in a desk, until the other day."

"You have not seen the young lady."

"No; he is to bring her to-morrow."

"And what sort of a man is this American? Is he a gentleman?"

"Well, I do not quite know. Perhaps Americans are different from Englishmen. If he was an Englishman, I should say without any hesitation that he is not a gentleman, as we count good breeding and good manners. He is a big man, handsome and burly, and he seems good-tempered. When I told him what was the full amount of Iris's inheritance—"

"Iris's inheritance!" Arnold repeated. "I beg your pardon, Clara; pray go on; but it seems like a dream."

"He only laughed, and said he was glad she would have so much. The utmost they hoped, he said, was that it might be a farm, or a house or two, or a few hundreds in the stocks. He is to bring her to-morrow, and of course I shall make her stay with me. As for himself, he says that he is only anxious to get back home to his wife and his practice."

"He wants nothing for himself, then? That seems a good sign."

"I asked him that question, and he said that he could not possibly take money for what he and his family had done for Iris; that is to say, her education and maintenance. This was very generous of him. Perhaps he is really a gentleman by birth, but has provincial manners. He said, however, that he had no objection to receiving the small amount of money spent on the voyage and on Iris's outfit, because they were not rich people, and it was a serious thing to fit out a young lady suitably. So of course I gave him what he suggested, a check for two hundred pounds. No one, he added with true feeling, would grudge a single dollar that had been spent upon the education of the dear girl; and this went to my heart."

"She is well educated, then?"

"She sings well," he says, "and has had a good plain education. He said I might rest assured that she was ladylike, because she had been brought up among his own friends."

"That is a very safe guarantee," said Arnold, laughing. "I wonder if she is pretty?"

"I asked him that question too, and he replied very oddly that she had a most splendid figure, which fetched everybody. Is not that rather a vulgar expression?"

"It is, in England. Perhaps in America it belongs to the first circles, and is a survival of the Pilgrim Fathers. So you gave him a check for two hundred pounds?"

"Yes; surely I was not wrong, Arnold. Consider the circumstances, the outfit and the voyage, and the man's reluctance and delicacy of feeling."

"I dare say you were quite right, but—well, I think I should have seen the young lady first. Remember, you have given the money to a stranger, on his bare word."

"Oh, Arnold, this man is perfectly honest. I would answer for his truth and honesty. He has frank, honest eyes. Besides, he brought me all those letters. Well, dear, you are not going to desert me because you are engaged, are you, Arnold? I want you to be present when she comes to-morrow morning."

"Certainly I will be present, with the greatest—no, not the greatest pleasure. But I will be present—I will come to luncheon, Clara."

When she was gone he thought again of the strange coincidence, both of the man and of the inheritance. Yet what had his Iris in common with a girl who had been brought up in America? Besides, she had lost her inheritance, and this other Iris had crossed the ocean to receive hers. Yet a very strange coincidence. It was so strange that he told it to Iris and to Lala Roy. Iris laughed, and said she did not know she had a single namesake. Lala did not laugh; but he sat thinking in silence. There was no chess for him that night; instead of playing his usual game, Mr. Emblem, in his chair, laughed and chuckled in rather a ghastly way.

CHAPTER X

"IT IS MY COUSIN"

"Well, Joe," said his wife, "and how is it going to finish? It looks to me as if there was a prison-van and a police-court at the end. Don't you think we had better back out of it while there is time?"

"You're a fool!" her husband replied—it was the morning after his visit to Clara; "you know nothing about it. Now listen."

"I do nothing but listen; you've told me the story till I know it by heart. Do you think anybody in the world will be so green as to believe such a clumsy plan as that?"

"Now look here, Lotty; if there's another word said—mind, now—you shall have nothing more to do with the business at all. I'll give it to a girl I know—a clever girl, who will carry it through with flying colors."

She set her lips hard, and drummed her fingers on the table. He knew how to rule his wife.

"Go on," she said, "since we can't be honest."

"Be reasonable, then; that's all I ask you. Honest! who is honest? Ain't we every one engaged in getting round our neighbors? Isn't the whole game, all the world over, lying and deceit? Honest! you might as well go on the boards without faking up your face, as try to live honest. Hold your tongue, then." He growled and swore, and after his fashion called on the Heavens to witness and express their astonishment.

The girl bent her head, and made no reply for a space. She was cowed and afraid. Presently she looked up and laughed, but with a forced laugh.

"Don't be cross, Joe; I'll do whatever you want me to do, and cheerfully, too, if it will do you any good. What is a woman good for but to help her husband? Only don't be cross, Joe."

She knew what her husband was by this time—a false and unscrupulous man. Yet she loved him. The case is not rare by any means, so that there is hope for all of us, from the meanest and most wriggling worm among us to the most hectoring ruffian.

"Why there, Lotty," he said, "that is what I like. Now listen. The old lady is a cake—do you understand? She is a sponge, she swallows everything, and is ready to fall on your neck and cry over you for joy. As for doubt or suspicion, not a word. I don't think there will be a single question asked. No, it's all 'My poor dear Claude'—that's your father, Lotty—and 'My poor dear Iris'—that's you, Lotty."

"All right, Joe, go on. I am Iris—I am anybody you like. Go on."

"The more I think about it, the more I'm certain we shall do the trick. Only keep cool over the job and forget the music-hall. You are Iris Deseret, and you are the daughter of Claude Deseret, deceased. I am Dr. Washington, one of the American family who brought you up. You're grateful, mind. Nothing can be more lively than your gratitude. We've been brother and sister, you and me, and I've got a wife and young family and a rising practice at home in the State of Maine, and I am only come over here to see you into your rights at great personal expense. Paid a substitute. Yes, actually paid a substitute. We only found the papers the other day, which is the reason why we did not come over before, and I am going home again directly."

"You are not really going away, Joe, are you?"

"No, I am going to stay here; but I shall pretend to go away. Now remember, we've got no suspicion ourselves, and we don't expect to meet any. If there is any, we are surprised and sorry. We don't come to the lady with a lawyer or a blunderbuss; we come as friends, and we shall arrange this little business between ourselves. Oh, never you fear, we shall arrange it quite comfortably, without lawyers."

"How much do you think we shall get out of it, Joe?"

"Listen, and open your eyes. There's nearly a hundred and twenty thousand pounds and a small estate in the country. Don't let us trouble about the estate more than we can help. Estates mean lawyers. Money doesn't."

He spoke as if small sums like a hundred thousand pounds are carried about in the pocket.

"Good gracious! And you've got two hundred of it already, haven't you?"

"Yes, but what is two hundred out of a hundred and twenty thousand? A hundred and twenty thousand! There's spending in it, isn't there, Lotty? Gad, we'll make the money spin, I calculate! It may be a few weeks before the old lady transfers the money—I don't quite know where it is, but in stocks or something—to your name. As soon as it is in your name I've got a plan. We'll remember that you've got a sweetheart or something in America, and you'll break your heart for wanting to see him. And then nothing will do but you must run across for a trip. Oh, I'll manage, and we'll make the money fly."

He was always adding new details to his story, finding

something to embellish it and heighten the effect, and now having succeeded in getting the false Iris into the house, he began already to devise schemes to get her out again.

"A hundred thousand pounds? Why, Joe, it is a terrible great sum of money. Good gracious! What shall we do with it, when we get it?"

"I'll show you what to do with it, my girl."

"And you said, Joe—you declared that it is your own by rights."

"Certainly it is my own. It would have been bequeathed to me by my own cousin. But she didn't know it. And she died without knowing it, and I am her heir."

Lotty wondered vaguely and rather sadly how much of this statement was true. But she did not dare to ask. She had promised her assistance. Every night she woke with a dreadful dream of a policeman knocking at the door; whenever she saw a man in blue she trembled; and she knew perfectly well that, if the plot failed, it was she herself, in all probability, and not her husband at all, who would be put in the dock. She did not believe a word about the cousin; she knew she was going to do a vile and dreadful wickedness, but she was ready to go through with it, or with anything else, to pleasure a husband who already, the honeymoon hardly finished, showed the propensities of a rover.

"Very well, Lotty; we are going there at once. You need take nothing with you, but you won't come back here for a good spell. In fact, I think I shall have to give up these lodgings, for fear of accidents. I shall leave you with your cousin."

"Yes; and I'm to be quiet, and behave pretty, I suppose?"

"You'll be just as quiet and demure as you used to be when you were serving in the music shop. No loud laughing, no capers, no comic songs, and no dancing."

"And am I to begin at once by asking for the money to be—what do you call it, transferred?"

"No; you are not on any account to say a word about the money; you are to go on living there without hinting at the money—without showing any desire to discuss the subject—perhaps for months, until there can't be the shadow of a doubt that you are the old woman's cousin. You are to make much of her, flatter her, cocker her up, find out all the family secrets, and get the length of her foot; but you are not to say one single word about the money. As for your manners, I'm not afraid of them, because when you like, you can look and talk like a countess."

"I know now." She got up and changed her face so that it became at once subdued and quiet, like a quiet serving-girl behind a counter. "So, is that modest enough, Joe? And as for singing, I shall sing for her, but not music-hall trash. This kind of thing. Listen."

There was a piano in the room, and she sat down and sang to her own accompaniment, with a sweet, low voice, one of the soft, sad German songs.

"That'll do," cried Joe. "Hang me! what a clever girl you are, Lotty! That's the kind of thing the swells like. As for me, give me ten minutes of Jolly Nash. But you know how to pull 'em in, Lotty."

It was approaching twelve, the hour when they were due. Lotty retired and arrayed herself in her quietest and most sober dress, a costume in some brown stuff, with a bonnet to match. She put on her best gloves and boots, having herself felt the inferiority of the shop-girl to the lady in those minor points, and she modified and mitigated her fringe, which, she knew, was rather more exaggerated than young ladies in society generally wear.

"You're not afraid, Lotty?" said Joe, when at last she was ready to start.

"Afraid? Not I, Joe. Come along. I couldn't look quieter, not if I was to make up as I do in the evening as a Quakeress. Come along. Oh, Joe, it will be awful dull! Don't forget to send word to the hall that I am ill. Afraid? Not I!" She laughed, but rather hysterically.

There would be, however, she secretly considered, some excitement when it came to the finding out, which would happen, she was convinced, in a very few hours. In fact, she had no faith at all in the story being accepted and believed by anybody; to be sure, she herself had been trained, as ladies in shops generally are, to mistrust all mankind, and she could not understand at all the kind of confidence which comes of having the very thing presented to you which you ardently desire. When they arrived in Chester Square, she found waiting for her a lady, who was certainly not beautiful, but she had kind eyes, which looked eagerly at the strange face, and with an expression of disappointment.

"It can't be the fringe," thought Lotty.

"Cousin Clara," she said softly and sweetly, as her husband had taught her, "I am Iris Deseret, the daughter of your old playfellow, Claude."

"Oh, my dear, my dear," cried Clara with enthusiasm, "come to my arms! Welcome home again!"

She kissed and embraced her. Then she held her by both hands, and looked at her face again.

"My dear," she said, "you have been a long time coming. I had almost given up hoping that Claude had any children. But you are welcome, after all—very welcome. You are in your own house, remember, my dear. This house is yours, and the plate, and furniture, and everything, and I am only your tenant."

"Oh!" said Lotty, overwhelmed. Why, she had actually been taken on her word, or rather the word of Joe.

"Let me kiss you again. Your face does not remind me as yet, in any single feature, of your father's. But I dare say I shall find resemblance presently. And indeed, your voice does remind me of him already. He had a singularly sweet and delicate voice."

"Iris has a remarkably sweet and delicate voice," said Joe, softly. "No doubt she got it from her father. You will hear her sing presently."

Lotty hardly knew her husband. His face was preternaturally solemn, and he looked as if he was engaged in the most serious business of his life.

"All her father's ways were gentle and delicate," said Clara.

"Just like hers," said Joe. "When all of us—American boys and girls, pretty rough at times—were playing and larking about, Iris would be just sittin' out like a cat on a carpet, quiet and demure. I suppose she got that way, too, from her father."

"No doubt; and as for your face, my dear, I dare say I shall find a likeness presently. But just now I see none. Will you take off your bonnet?"

When the girl's bonnet was off, Clara looked at her again, curiously, but kindly.

"I suppose I can't help looking for a likeness, my dear. But you must take after your mother, whom I never saw. Your father's eyes were full and limpid; yours are large, and clear, and bright; very good eyes, my dear, but they are not limpid. His mouth was flexible and mobile, but yours is firm. Your hair, however, reminds me somewhat of his, which was much your light shade of brown when he was young. And now, sir"—she addressed Joe—"now that you have brought this dear girl all the way across the Atlantic, what are you going to do?"

"Well, I don't exactly know that there's anything to keep me," said Joe. "You see, I've got my practice to look after at home—I am a physician, as I told you—and my wife and children; and the sooner I get back the better, now that I can leave Iris with her friends, safe and comfortable. Stay," he added, "there are all those papers which I promised you—the certificates, and the rest of them. You had better take them all, miss, and keep them for Iris."

"Thank you," said Clara, touched by this confidence; "Iris will be safe with me. It is very natural that you should want to go home again. And you will be content to stay with me, my dear, won't you? You need not be afraid, sir; I assure you that her interests will not in any way suffer. Tell her to write and let you know exactly what is done. Let her, however, since she is an English girl, remain with English friends, and get to know her cousins and relations. You can safely trust her with me, Dr. Washington."

"Thank you," said Joe. "You know that when one has known a girl all her life, one is naturally anxious about her happiness. We are almost brother and sister."

"I know; and I am sure, Mr. Washington, we ought to be most grateful to you. As for the money you have expended upon her, let me once more beg of you—"

Joe waved his hand majestically.

"As for that," he said, "the money is spent. Iris is welcome to it, if it were ten times as much. Now, madam, you trusted me, the very first day that you saw me, with two hundred pounds sterling. Only an English lady would have done that. You trusted me without asking me who or what I was, or doubting my word. I assure you, madam, I felt that kindness, and that trust, very much indeed, and in return, I have brought you Iris herself. After all expenses paid of coming over and getting back, buying a few things for Iris, if I find that there's anything over, I shall ask you to take back the balance. Madam, I thank you for the money, but I am sure I have repaid you—with Iris."

This was a very clever speech. If there had been a shadow of doubt before it in Clara's heart (which there was not), it would vanish now. She cordially and joyfully accepted her newly-found cousin.

"And now, Iris," he said with a manly tremor in his voice, "I do not know if I shall see you again before I go away. If not, I shall take your fond love to all of them at home—Tom, and Dick, and Harry, and Harriet, and Prissy, and all of them"—Joe really was carrying the thing through splendidly—"and perhaps, my dear, when you are a grand lady in England, you will give a thought—a thought now and again—to your old friends across the water."

"Oh, Joe!" cried Lotty, really carried away with admiration, and ashamed of her skeptical spirit. "Oh," she whispered, "ain't you splendid!"

"But you must not go, Dr. Washington," said Clara, "without coming again to say farewell. Will you not dine with us to-night? Will you stay and have lunch?"

"No, madam, I thank you. It will be best for me to leave Iris alone with you. The sooner she learns your English ways and forgets American ways, the better."

"But you are not going to start away for Liverpool at once? You will stay a day or two in London—"

The American physician said that perhaps he might stay a week longer for scientific purposes.

"Have you got enough money, Joe?" asked the new Iris thoughtfully.

Joe gave her a glance of infinite admiration.

"Well," he said, "the fact is that I should like to buy a few books and things. Perhaps—"

"Cousin," said Lotty eagerly, "please give him a check for a hundred pounds. Make it a hundred. You said everything was mine. No, Joe, I won't hear a word about repayment, as if a little thing like fifty pounds, or a hundred pounds, should want to be repaid! As if you and I could ever talk about repayment!"

Clara did as she was asked readily and eagerly. Then Joe departed, promising to call and say farewell before he left England, and resolving that in his next visit—his last visit—there should be another check. But he had made one mistake; he had parted with the papers. No one in any situation of life should ever give up the power, until he has secured the substance. But it is human to err.

"And now, my dear," said Clara warmly, "sit down and let us talk. Arnold is coming to lunch with us, and to make your acquaintance."

When Arnold came a few minutes later, he was astonished to find his cousin already on the most affectionate terms with the newly-arrived Iris Deseret. She was walking about the room showing her the pictures of her grandfather and other ancestors, and they were hand-in-hand.

"Arnold," said Clara, "this is Iris, and I hope you will both be great friends; Iris, this is my cousin, but he is not yours."

"I don't pretend to know how that may be," said the young lady. "But then I am glad to know all your cousins, whether they are mine or not; only don't bother me with questions, because I don't remember anything, and I don't know anything. Why, until the other day I did not even know that I was an English lady, not until they found those papers."

A strange accent for an American! and she certainly said "laidy" for "lady," and "paipper" for "paper," like a cockney. Alas! This comes of London Music Halls even to country-bred damsels!

Arnold made a mental observation that the new-comer might be called anything in the world, but could not be called a lady. She was handsome, certainly, but how could Claude Deseret's daughter have grown into so common a type of beauty? Where was the delicacy of feature and manner which Clara had never ceased to commend in speaking of her lost cousin?

"Iris," said Clara, "is our little savage from the American Forest. She is Queen Pocahontas, who has come over to conquer England and to win all our hearts. My dear, my Cousin Arnold will help me to make you an English girl."

She spoke as in the State of Maine was still the hunting-ground of Sioux and Iroquois.

Arnold thought that a less American-looking girl he had never seen; that she did not speak or look like a lady was to be expected, perhaps, if she had, as was probable, been brought up by rough and unpolished people. But he had no doubt, any more than Clara herself, as to the identity of the girl. Nobody ever doubts a claimant. Every impostor, from Demetrius downward, has gained his supporters and partisans by simply living among them and keeping up the imposition. It is so easy, in fact, to be a claimant, that it is wonderful there are not more of them.

Then luncheon was served, and the young lady not only showed a noble appetite, but to Arnold's astonishment, confessed to an ardent love for bottled stout.

"Most American ladies," he said impertinently, "only drink water, do they not?"

Lotty perceived that she had made a mistake.

"I only drink stout," she said, "when the doctor tells me. But I like it all the same."

She certainly had no American accent. But she would not talk much; she was, perhaps, shy. After luncheon, however, Clara asked her if she would sing, and she complied, showing considerable skill with her accompaniment, and singing a simple song in good taste and with a sweet voice. Arnold observed, however, that there was some weakness about the letter "h," less common among Americans than among the English. Presently he went away, and the girl, who had been aware that he was watching her, breathed more easily.

"Who is your Cousin Arnold?" she asked.

"My dear, he is my cousin but not yours. You will not see him often, because he is going to be married, I am sorry to say, and to be married beneath him—oh, it is dreadful! to some tradesman's girl, my dear."

"Dreadful!" said Iris with a queer look in her eyes. "Well, cousin, I don't want to see much of him. He's a good-looking chap, too, though rather too finicking for my taste. I like a man who looks as if he could knock another man down. Besides, he looks at me as if I was a riddle, and he wanted to find out the answer."

In the evening Arnold found that no change had come over the old man. He was, however, perfectly happy, so that, considering the ruin of his worldly prospects, it was, perhaps, as well that he had parted, for a time, at least, with his wits. Some worldly misfortunes there are which should always produce this effect.

"You told me," said Lala Roy, "that another Iris had just come from America to claim an inheritance of your cousin."

"Yes; it is a very strange coincidence."

"Very strange. Two Englishmen die in America at the same time, each having a daughter named Iris, and each daughter entitled to some kind of inheritance."

Lala Roy spoke slowly, and with meaning.

"Oh!" cried Arnold. "It is more than strange. Do you think— is it possible—"

He could not for the moment clothe his thoughts in words.

"Do you know if any one has brought this girl to England?"

"Yes; she was brought over by a young American physician, one of the family who adopted and brought her up."

"What is he like—the young American physician?"

"I have not seen him."

"Go, my young friend, to-morrow morning, and ask your cousin if this photograph resembles the American physician."

It was the photograph of a handsome young fellow, with strongly marked features, apparently tall and well-set-up.

"Lala, you don't really suspect anything—you don't think—"

"Hush! I know who has stolen the papers. Perhaps the same man has produced the heiress."

"And you think—you suspect that the man who stole the papers is connected with—But then those papers must be— oh, it cannot be! For then Iris would be Clara's cousin— Clara's cousin—and the other an impostor."

"Even so; everything is possible. But silence. Do not speak a word, even to Iris. If the papers are lost, they are lost. Say nothing to her yet; but go—go, and find out if that photograph resembles the American physician. The river wanders here and there, but the sea swallows it at last."

Walter Besant

CHAPTER XI

MR. JAMES MAKES ATONEMENT

James arrived as usual in the morning at nine o'clock, in order to take down the shutters. To his astonishment, he found Lala Roy and Iris waiting for him in the back shop. And they had grave faces.

"James," said Iris, "your master has suffered a great shock, and is not himself this morning. His safe has been broken open by some one, and most important papers have been taken out."

"Papers, miss—papers? Out of the safe?"

"Yes. They are papers of no value whatever to the thief, whoever he may be. But they are of the very greatest importance to us. Your master seems to have lost his memory for a while, and cannot help us in finding out who has done this wicked thing. You have been a faithful servant for so long that I am sure you will do what you can for us. Think for us. Try to remember if anybody besides yourself has had access to this room when your master was out of it."

James sat down. He felt that he must sit down, though Lala Roy was looking at him with eyes full of doubt and suspicion. The whole enormity of his own guilt, though he had not stolen anything, fell upon him. He had got the key; he had given it to Mr. Joseph; and he had received it back again. In fact, at that very moment, it was lying in his pocket. The worst that he had feared had happened. The safe was robbed.

He was struck with so horrible a dread, and so fearful a looking forward to judgment and condemnation, that his teeth chattered and his eye gave way.

"You will think it over, James," said Iris; "think it over, and tell us presently if you can remember anything."

"Think it over, Mr. James," Lala Roy repeated in his deepest tone, and with an emphatic gesture of his right forefinger. "Think it over carefully. Like a lamp that is never extinguished are the eyes of the faithful servant."

They left him, and James fell back into his chair with hollow cheek and beating heart.

"He told me," he murmured—"oh, the villain!—he swore to me that he had taken nothing from the safe. He said he only looked in it, and read the contents. The scoundrel! He has stolen the papers! He must have known they were there. And then, to save himself, he put me on to the job. For who would be suspected if not—oh, Lord!—if not me?"

He grasped his paste brush, and attacked his work with a feverish anxiety to find relief in exertion; but his heart was not in it, and presently a thought pierced his brain, as an arrow pierceth the heart, and under the pang and agony of it, his face turned ashy-pale, and the big drops stood upon his brow.

"For," he thought, "suppose that the thing gets abroad; suppose they were to advertise a reward; suppose the man who made the key were to see the advertisement or to hear about it! And he knows my name, too, and my business; and he'll let out for a reward—I know he will—who it was ordered that key of him."

Already he saw himself examined before a magistrate; already he saw in imagination that locksmith's man who made the key kissing the Testament, and giving his testimony in clear and distinct words, which could not be shaken.

"Oh, Lord! oh, Lord!" he groaned. "No one will believe me, even if I do confess the truth: and as for him, I know him well; if I go to him, he'll only laugh at me. But I must go to him—I must!"

He was so goaded by his terror that he left the shop unprotected—a thing he had never thought to do—and ran as fast as he could to Joe's lodgings. But he had left them; he was no longer there; he had not been there for six weeks; the landlady did not know his address, or would not give it. Then James felt sick and dizzy, and would have sat down on the doorstep and cried but for the look of the thing. Besides, he remembered the unprotected shop. So he turned away sadly and walked back, well understanding now that he had fallen like a tool into a trap, artfully set to fasten suspicion and guilt upon himself.

When he returned he found the place full of people. Mr. Emblem was sitting in his customary place, and he was smiling. He did not look in the least like a man who had been robbed. He was smiling pleasantly and cheerfully. Mr. Chalker was also present, a man with whom no one ever smiled, and Lala Roy, solemn and dignified, and a man—an unknown man—who sat in the outer shop, and seemed to take no interest at all in the proceedings. Were they come, he asked himself, to arrest him on the spot?

Apparently they were not, for no one took the least notice of him, and they were occupied with something else. How could they think of anything else? Yet Mr. Chalker, standing at the table, was making a speech, which had nothing to do with the robbery.

"Here I am, you see, Mr. Emblem," he said; "I have told you already that I don't want to do anything to worry you. Let us be friends all round. This gentleman, your friend from India, will advise you, I am sure, for your own good, not to be obstinate. Lord! what is the amount, after all, to a substantial man like yourself? A substantial man, I say." He spoke confidently, but he glanced about the shop with doubtful eyes. "Granted that it was borrowed to get your grandson out of a scrape—supposing he promised to pay it back and hasn't done so; putting the case that it has grown and developed itself as bills will do, and can't help doing, and can't be stopped; it isn't the fault of the lawyers, but the very nature of a hill to go on growing—it's like a baby for growing. Why, after all, you were your grandson's security—you can't escape that. And when I would no longer renew, you gave of your own accord—come now, you can't deny that—a Bill of Sale on goods and furniture. Now, Mr. Emblem, didn't, you? Don't let us have any bitterness or quarreling. Let's be friends, and tell me I may send away the man."

Mr. Emblem smiled pleasantly, but did not reply.

"A Bill of Sale it was, dated January the 25th, 1883, just before that cursed Act of Parliament granted the five days' notice. Here is the bailiff's man in possession. You can pay the amount, which is, with costs and Sheriff's Poundage, three hundred and fifty-one pounds thirteen shillings and fourpence, at once, or you may pay it five days hence. Otherwise the shop, and furniture, and all, will be sold off in seven days."

"Oh," James gasped, listening with bewilderment, "we can't be going to be sold up! Emblem's to be sold up!"

"Three hundred and fifty pounds!" said Mr. Emblem. "My friend, let us rather speak of thousands. This is a truly happy day for all of us. Sit down, Mr. Chalker—my dear friend, sit down. Rejoice with us. A happy morning."

"What the devil is the matter with him?" asked the money-lender.

"There was something, Mr. Chalker," Mr. Emblem went on

cheerfully, "something said about my grandson. Joe was always a bad lot; lucky his father and mother are out of the way in Australia. You came to me about that business, perhaps? Oh, on such a joyful day as this I forgive everybody. Tell Joe I do not want to see him, but I have forgiven him."

"Oh, he's mad!" growled James; "he's gone stark staring mad!"

"You don't seem quite yourself this morning, Mr. Emblem," said Mr. Chalker. "Perhaps this gentleman, your friend from India, will advise you when I am gone. You don't understand, Mister," he addressed Lala Roy, "the nature of a bill. Once you start a bill, and begin to renew it, it's like planting a tree, for it grows and grows of its own accord, and by Act of Parliament, too, though they do try to hack and cut it down in the most cruel way. You see Mr. Emblem is obstinate. He's got to pay off that bill, which is a Bill of Sale, and he won't do it. Make him write the check and have done with it."

"This is the best day's work I ever did," Mr. Emblem went on. "To remember the letter, word for word, and everything! Mr. Arbuthnot has, very likely, finished the whole business by now. Thousands—thousands—and all for Iris!"

"Look here, Mr. Emblem," said the lawyer angrily. "You'll not only be a bankrupt if you go on like this, but you'll be a fraudulent bankrupt as well. Is it honest, I want to know, to refuse to pay your just debts when you've put by thousands, as you boast—you actually boast—for your granddaughter?"

"Yes," said the old man, "Iris will have thousands."

"I think, sir," said Lala Roy, "that you are under an illusion. Mr. Emblem does not possess any such savings or investments as you imagine."

"Then why does he go on talking about thousands?"

"He has had a shock; he cannot quite understand what has

happened. You had better leave him for the present."

"Leave him! And nothing but these moldy old books! Here, you sir—you James—you shopman—come here! What is the stock worth?"

"It depends upon whether you are buying or selling," said James. "If you were to sell it under the hammer, in lots, it wouldn't fetch a hundred pounds."

"There, you hear—you hear, all of you! Not a hundred pounds, and my Bill of Sale is three-fifty."

"Pray, sir," said Lala Roy, "who told you that Mr. Emblem was so wealthy?"

"His grandson."

"Then, sir perhaps it would be well to question the grandson further, he may know things of which we have heard nothing."

The Act of 1882, which came into operation in the following January, is cruel indeed, I am told, to those who advanced money on Bills of Sale before that date, for it allows—it actually allows the debtor five clear days during which he may, if he can, without being caught, make away with portions of his furniture and belongings—the smaller and the more precious portion; or he may find some one else to lend him the money, and so get off clear and save his sticks. It is, as the modern Shylock declares, a most wicked and iniquitous Act, by which the shark may be balked, and many an honest tradesman, who would otherwise have been most justly ruined, is enabled to save his stock, and left to worry along until the times become more prosperous. To a man like Mr. David Chalker, such an Act of Parliament is most revolting.

He went away at length, leaving the man—the professional person—behind. Then Lala Roy persuaded Mr. Emblem to go upstairs again. He did so without any apparent consciousness that there was a Man in Possession.

"James," said Lala Roy, "you have heard that your master has been robbed. You are reflecting and meditating on this circumstance. Another thing is that a creditor has threatened to sell off everything for a debt. Most likely, everything will be sold, and the shop closed. You will, therefore, lose the place you have had for five-and-twenty years. That is a very bad business for you. You are unfortunate this morning. To lose your place—and then this robbery. That seems also a bad business."

"It is," said James with a hollow groan. "It is, Mr. Lala Roy. It is a dreadful bad business."

"Pray, Mr. James," continued this man with grave, searching eyes which made sinners shake in their shoes, "pray, why did you run away, and where did you go after you opened the shop this morning? You went to see Mr. Emblem's grandson, did you not?"

"Yes, I did," said James.

"Why did you go to see him?"

"I w—w—went—oh, Lord!—I went to tell him what had happened, because he is master's grandson, and I thought he ought to know," said James.

"Did you tell him?"

"No; he has left his lodgings. I don't know where he is—oh, and he always told me the shop was his—settled on him," he said.

"He is the Father of Lies; his end will be confusion. Shame and confusion shall wait upon all who have hearkened unto him or worked with him, until they repent and make atonement."

"Don't, Mister Lala Roy—don't; you frighten me," said James. "Oh, what a dreadful liar he is!"

All the morning the philosopher sat in the bookseller's chair, and James, in the outer shop, felt that those deep eyes were resting continually upon him, and knew that bit by bit his secret would be dragged from him. If he could get up and run away—if a customer would come—if the dark gentleman would go upstairs—if he could think of something else! But none of these things happened, and James, at his table with the paste before him, passed a morning compared with which any seat anywhere in Purgatory would have been comfortable. Presently a strange feeling came over him, as if some invisible force was pushing and dragging him and forcing him to leave his chair, and throw himself at the Philosopher's feet and confess everything. This was the mesmeric effect of those reproachful eyes fixed steadily upon him. And in the doorway, like some figure in a nightmare—a figure incongruous and out of place—the Man in Possession sitting, passive and unconcerned, with one eye on the street and the other on the shop. Upstairs Mr. Emblem was sitting fast asleep; joy had made him sleepy; and Iris was at work among her pupils' letters, compiling sums for the Fruiterer, making a paper on Conic Sections for the Cambridge man, and working out Trigonometrical Equations for the young schoolmaster, and her mind full of a solemn exultation and glory, for she was a woman who was loved. The other things troubled her but little. Her grandfather would get back his equilibrium of mind; the shop might be shut up, but that mattered little. Arnold, and Lala Roy, and her grandfather, and herself, would all live together, and she and Arnold would work. The selfishness of youth is really astonishing. Nothing—except perhaps toothache—can make a girl unhappy who is loved and newly betrothed. She may say what she pleases, and her face may be a yard long when she speaks of the misfortunes of others, but all the time her heart is dancing.

To Lala Roy, the situation presented a problem with insufficient data, some of which would have to be guessed. A

Walter Besant

letter, now lost, said that a certain case contained papers necessary to obtain an unknown inheritance for Iris. How then to ascertain whether anybody was expecting or looking for a girl to claim an inheritance? Then there was half a coat-of-arms, and lastly there was a certain customer of unknown name, who had been acquainted with Iris's father before his marriage. So far for Iris. As for the thief, Lala Roy had no doubt at all. It was, he was quite certain, the grandson, whose career he had watched for some years with interest and curiosity. Who else was there who would steal the papers? And who would help him, and give him access to the safe? He did not only suspect, he was certain that James was in some way cognizant of the deed. Why else did he turn so pale? Why did he rush off to Joe's lodgings? Why did he sit trembling?

At half-past twelve Lala Roy rose.

"It is your dinner-hour," he said to James, and it seemed to the unhappy man as it he was saying, "I know all." "It is your dinner hour; go, eat, refresh the body. Whom should suspicion affright except the guilty?"

James put on his hat and sneaked—he felt that he was sneaking—out of the shop.

During his dinner-hour, Joseph himself called. It was an unusual thing to see him at any time; in fact, as he was never wont to call upon his grandfather, unless he was in a scrape and wanted money, no one ever made the poor young man welcome, or begged him to come more often.

But this morning, he walked upstairs and appeared so cheerful, so entirely free from any self-reproach for past sins, and so easy in his mind, without the least touch of the old hang-dog look, that Iris began to reproach herself for thinking badly of her cousin.

When he was told about the robbery, he expressed the greatest surprise that any one in the world could be so wicked as to rob an old man like his grandfather. Besides his abhorrence of crime in the abstract, he affirmed that the robbery of a safe was a species of villainy for which hanging was too mild—much too mild a punishment. He then asked his grandfather what were the contents of the packet stolen, and when he received no answer except a pleasant and a cheery laugh, he asked Iris, and learned to his sorrow that the contents were unknown, and could not, therefore, be identified even if they were found. This, he said, was a thousand pities, because, if they had been known, a reward might have been offered. For his own part he would advise the greatest caution. Nothing at all should be done at first; no step should be taken which might awaken suspicion; they should go on as if the papers were without value. As for that, they had no real proof that there was any robbery. Iris thought of telling him about the water-mark of the blank pages, but refrained. Perhaps there was no robbery after all—who was to prove what had been inside the packet? But if there had been papers, and it they were valueless except to the rightful owners, they would, perhaps, be sent back voluntarily; or after a time, say a year or two, they might be advertised for; not as if the owners were very anxious to get them, and not revealing the nature of the papers, but cautiously; and presently, if they had not been destroyed, the holders of the papers would answer the advertisement, and then a moderate reward might, after a while, be offered; and so on, giving excellent advice. While he was speaking, Lala Roy entered the room in his noiseless manner, and took his accustomed chair.

"And what do you think, sir?" said Joseph, when he had finished. "You have heard my advice. You are not an Englishman, but I suppose you've got some intelligence."

Lala bowed and spread his hands, but replied not.

"Your opinion should be asked," Joseph went on, "because you see, as the only other person, besides my grandfather and my cousin, in the house, you might yourself be suspected. Indeed," he added, "I have no doubt you will be suspected. When I talk over the conduct of the case, which will be my task, I suppose, it will, perhaps, be my duty to suspect you."

Lala bowed again and again, spread his hands, but did not speak.

In fact, Joseph now perceived that he was having the conversation wholly to himself. His grandfather sat passive, listening as one who, in a dream, hears voices but does not heed what they are saying, yet smiling politely. Iris listened, but paid no heed. She thought that a great deal of fuss was being made about papers, which, perhaps, were worth nothing. And as for her inheritance, why, as she never expected to get any, she was not going to mourn the loss of what, perhaps, was worth nothing.

"Very well, then," said Joseph, "that's all I've got to say. I've given you the best advice I can, and I suppose I may go. Have you lost your voice, Iris?"

"No; but I think you had better go, Joseph. My grandfather is not able to talk this morning, and I dare say your advice is very good, but we have other advisers."

"As for you, Mr. Lala Roy, or whatever you call yourself," said Joe roughly, "I've warned you. Suspicion certainly will fall upon you, and what I say is—take care. For my own part I never did believe in niggers, and I wouldn't have one in my house."

Lala Roy bowed again and spread his fingers.

Then Joseph went away. The door between the shop and the hall was half open, and he looked in. A strange man was sitting in the outer shop, a pipe in his mouth, and James was leaning his head upon his hands, with wild and haggard eyes gazing straight before him.

"Poor devil," murmured Joseph. "I feel for him, I do indeed.

He had the key made—for himself; he certainly let me use it once, but only once, and who's to prove it? And he's had the opportunity every day of using it himself. That's very awkward, Foxy, my boy. If I were Foxy, I should be in a funk, myself."

He strolled away, thinking that all promised well. Lotty most favorably and unsuspiciously received in her new character; no one knowing the contents of the packet; his grandfather gone silly; and for himself, he had had the opportunity of advising exactly what he wished to be done—namely, that silence and inaction should be observed for a space, in order to give the holders of the property a chance of offering terms. What better advice could he give? And what line of action would be better or safer for himself?

If James had known who was in the house-passage, the other side of the door, there would, I think, have been a collision of two solid bodies. But he did not know, and presently Lala Roy came back, and the torture began again. James took down books and put them up again; he moved about feverishly, doing nothing, with a duster in his hand; but all the time he felt those deep accusing eyes upon him with a silence worse than a thousand questions. He knew—he was perfectly certain—that he should be found out. And all the trouble for nothing! and the Bailiff's man in possession, and the safe robbed, and those eyes upon him, saying, as plain as eyes could speak, "Thou art the Man!"

"And Joe is the man," said James; "not me at all. What I did was wrong, but I was tempted. Oh, what a precious liar and villain he is! And what a fool I've been!"

The day passed more slowly than it seemed possible for any day to pass; always the man in the shop; always the deep eyes of the silent Hindoo upon him. It was a relief when, once, Mr. Chalker looked in and surveyed the shelves with a suspicious air, and asked if the old man had by this time listened to reason.

It is the business of him who makes plunder out of other men's distresses—as the jackal feeds upon the offal and the putrid carcass—to know as exactly as he can how his fellow-creatures are situated. For this reason such a one doth diligently inquire, listen, pick up secrets, put two and two together, and pry curiously into everybody's affairs, being never so happy as when he gets an opportunity of going to the rescue of a sinking man. Thus among those who lived in good repute about the lower end of the King's Road, none had a better name than Mr. Emblem, and no one was considered to have made more of his chances. And it was with joy that Mr. Chalker received Joe one evening and heard from him the dismal story, that if he could not find fifty pounds within a few hours, he was ruined. The fifty pounds was raised on a bill bearing Mr. Emblem's name. When it was presented, however, and the circumstances explained, the old gentleman, who had at first refused to own the signature, accepted it meekly, and told no one that his grandson had written it himself, without the polite formality of asking permission to sign for him. In other words Joseph was a forger, and Mr. Chalker knew it, and this made him the more astonished when Mr. Emblem did not take up the bill, but got it renewed quarter after quarter, substituting at length a bill of sale, as if he was determined to pay as much as possible for his grandson's sins.

"Where is he?" asked the money-lender angrily. "Why doesn't he come down and face his creditors?"

"Master's upstairs," said James, "and you've seen yourself, Mr. Chalker, that he is off his chump. And oh, sir, who would have thought that Emblem's would have come to ruin?"

"But there's something, James—Come, think—there must be something."

"Mr. Joseph said there were thousands. But he's a terrible liar—oh, Mr. Chalker, he's a terrible liar and villain! Why, he's even deceived me!"

"What? Has he borrowed your money?"

"Worse—worse. Do you know where I could find him, sir?"

"Well, I don't know—" Mr. Chalker was not in the habit of giving addresses, but in this case, perhaps Joe might be squeezed as well as his grandfather. Unfortunately that bill with the signature had been destroyed. "I don't know. Perhaps if I find out I may tell you. And, James, if you can learn anything—this rubbish won't fetch half the money—I'll make it worth your while, James, I will indeed."

"I'll make him take his share," said James to himself. "If I have to go to prison, he shall go too. They sha'n't send me without sending him."

He looked round. The watchful eyes were gone. The Hindoo had gone away noiselessly. James breathed again.

"After all," he said, "how are they to find out? How are they to prove anything? Mr. Joseph took the things, and I helped him to a key; and he isn't likely to split, and—oh, Lord, if they were to find it!" For at that moment he felt the duplicate key in his waistcoat-pocket. "If they were to find it!"

He took the key out, and looked at the bright and innocent-looking thing, as a murderer might look at his blood stained dagger.

Just then, as he gazed upon it, holding it just twelve inches in front of his nose, one hand was laid upon his shoulder, and another took the key from between his fingers.

He turned quickly, and his knees gave way, and he sunk upon the floor, crying:

"Oh, Mr. Lala Roy, sir, Mr. Lala Roy, I am not the thief! I am innocent! I will tell you all about it! I will confess all to you! I will indeed! I will make atonement! Oh, what a miserable fool I've been!"

"Upon the heels of Folly," said the Sage, "treadeth Shame. You will now be able to understand the words of wisdom, which say of the wicked man, 'The curse of iniquity pursueth him; he liveth in continual fear; the anxiety of his mind taketh vengeance upon him.' Stand up and speak."

The Man in Possession looked on as if an incident of this kind was too common in families for him to take any notice of it. Nothing, in fact, is able to awaken astonishment in the heart of the Man in Possession, because nothing is sacred to him except the "sticks" he has to guard. To Iris, the event was, however, of importance, because it afforded Lala Roy a chance of giving Arnold that photograph, no other than an early portrait of Mr. Emblem's grandson.

CHAPTER XII

IS THIS HIS PHOTOGRAPH?

The best way to get a talk with his cousin was to dine with her. Arnold therefore went to Chester Square next day with the photograph in his pocket. It was half an hour before dinner when he arrived, and Clara was alone.

"My dear," she cried with enthusiasm, "I am charmed—I am delighted—with Iris."

"I am glad," said Arnold mendaciously.

"I am delighted with her—in every way. She is more and better than I could have expected—far more. A few Americanisms, of course—"

"No doubt," said Arnold. "When I saw her I thought they rather resembled Anglicisms. But you have had opportunities of judging. You have in your own possession," he continued, "have you not, all the papers which establish her identity?"

"Oh, yes; they are all locked up in my strong-box. I shall be very careful of them. Though, of course, there is no one who has to be satisfied except myself. And I am perfectly satisfied. But then I never had any doubt from the beginning. How could there be any doubt?"

"How, indeed?"

"Truth, honor, loyalty, and candor, as well as gentle descent, are written on that girl's noble brow, Arnold, plain, so that all may read. It is truly wonderful," she went on, "how the old gentle blood shows itself, and will break out under the most unexpected conditions. In her face she is not much like her father; that is true; though sometimes I catch a momentary resemblance, which instantly disappears again. Her eyes are not in the least like his, nor has she his manner, or carriage, or any of his little tricks and peculiarities—though, perhaps, I shall observe traces of some of them in time. But especially she resembles him in her voice. The tone—the timbre—reminds me every moment of my poor Claude."

"I suppose," said Arnold, "that one must inherit something, if it is only a voice, from one's father. Have you said anything to her yet about money matters, and a settlement of her claims?"

"No, not yet. I did venture, last night, to approach the subject, but she would not hear of it. So I dropped it. I call that true delicacy, Arnold—native, instinctive, hereditary delicacy."

"Have you given any more money to the American gentleman who brought her home?"

"Iris made him take a hundred pounds, against his will, to buy books with, for he is not rich. Poor fellow! It went much against the grain with him to take the money. But she made him take it. She said he wanted books and instruments, and insisted on his having at least a hundred pounds. It was generous of her. Yes; she is—I am convinced—a truly generous girl, and as open-handed as the day. Now, would a common girl, a girl of no descent, have shown so much delicacy and generosity?"

"By the way, Clara, here is a photograph. Does it belong to you? I—I picked it up."

He showed the photograph which Lala Roy had given him.

"Oh, yes; it is a likeness of Dr. Washington, Iris's adopted brother and guardian. She must have dropped it. I should think it was taken a few years back, but it is still a very good likeness. A handsome man, is he not? He grows upon one rather. His parting words with Iris yesterday were very dignified and touching."

"I will give it to her presently," he replied, without further comment.

There was, then, no doubt. The woman was an impostor, and the man was the thief, and the papers were the papers which had been stolen from the safe, and Iris Deseret was no other than his own Iris. But he must not show the least sign of suspicion.

"What are you thinking about, Arnold?" asked Clara. "Your face is as black as thunder. You are not sorry that Iris has returned, are you?"

"I was thinking of my engagement, Clara."

"Why, you are not tired of it already? An engaged man, Arnold, ought not to look so gloomy as that."

"I am not tired of it yet. But I am unhappy as regards some circumstances connected with it. Your disapproval, Clara, for one. My dear cousin, I owe so much to you, that I want to owe you more. Now, I have a proposition—a promise—to make to you. I am now so sure, so very sure and certain, that you will want me to marry Miss Aglen—and no one else—when you once know her, that I will engage solemnly not to marry her unless you entirely approve. Let me owe my wife to you, as well as everything else."

"Arnold, you are not in earnest."

"Quite in earnest."

"But I shall never approve. Never—never—never! I could not bring myself, under any circumstances that I can conceive, to approve of such a connection."

"My dear cousin, I am, on the other hand, perfectly certain that you will approve. Why, if I were not quite certain, do you think I should have made this promise? But to return to your newly-found cousin. Tell me more about her."

"Well, I have discovered that she is a really very clever and gifted girl. She can imitate people in the most wonderful way, especially actresses, though she has only been to a theater once or twice in her life. At Liverpool she heard some one sing what she calls a Tropical Song, and this she actually remembers— she carried it away in her head, every word—and she can sing it just as they sing it on the stage, with all the vulgarity and gestures imitated to the very life. Of course I should not like her to do this before anybody else, but it is really wonderful."

"Indeed!" said Arnold. "It must be very clever and amusing."

"Of course," said Clara, with colossal ignorance, "an American lady can hardly be expected to understand English vulgarities. No doubt there is an American variety."

Arnold thought that a vulgar song could be judged at its true value by any lady, either American or English, but he said nothing.

And then the young lady herself appeared. She had been driving about with Clara among various shops, and now bore upon her person the charming result of these journeys, in the shape of a garment, which was rich in texture, and splendid in the making. And she really was a handsome girl, only with a certain air of being dressed for the stage. But Arnold, now more than suspicious, was not dazzled by the gorgeous raiment, and only considered how his cousin could for a moment imagine this person to be a lady, and how it would be best to break the news.

"Clara's cousin," she said, "I have forgotten your name; but how do you do, again?"

And then they went in to dinner.

"You have learned, I suppose," said Arnold, "something about the Deseret family by this time?"

"Oh, yes, I have heard all about the family-tree. I dare say I shall get to know it by heart in time. But you don't expect me all at once, to care much for it."

"Little Republican!" said Clara. "She actually does not feel a pride in belonging to a good old family."

The girl made a little gesture.

"Your family can't do much for you, that I can see, except to make you proud, and pretend not to see other women in the shop. That is what the county ladies do."

"Why, my dear, what on earth do you know of the county ladies?"

Lotty blushed a little. She had made a mistake. But she quickly recovered.

"I only know what I've read, cousin, about any kind of English ladies. But that's enough, I'm sure. Stuck-up things!"

And again she observed, from Clara's pained expression, that she had made another mistake.

If she showed a liking for stout at lunch, she manifested a positive passion for champagne at dinner.

"I do like the English custom," she said, "of having two dinners in the day."

"Ladies in America, I suppose," said Clara, "dine in the middle of the day?"

"Always."

"But I have visited many families in New York and Boston who dined late," said Arnold.

"Dare say," she replied carelessly. "I'm going to have some more of that curry stuff, please. And don't ask any more questions, anybody, till I've worried through with it. I'm a wolf at curry."

"She likes England, Arnold," said Clara, covering up this remark, so to speak. "She likes the country, she says, very much."

"At all events," said the girl, "I like this house, which is first-class—fine—proper. And the furniture, and pictures, and all—tiptop. But I'm afraid it is going to be awful dull, except at meals, and when the Boy is going." Her own head was just touched by the "Boy," and she was a little off her guard.

"My dear child," said Clara, "you have only just come, and you have not yet learned to know and love your own home and your father's friends. You must take a little time."

"Oh, I'll take time. As long as you like. But I shall soon be tired of sitting at home. I want to go about and see things—theaters and music-halls, and all kinds of places."

"Ladies, in England, do not go to music-halls," said Arnold.

"Gentlemen do. Why not ladies, then? Answer me that. Why can't ladies go, when gentlemen go? What is proper for gentlemen is proper for ladies. Very well, then, I want to go somewhere every night. I want to see everything there is to see, and to hear all that there is to hear."

"We shall go, presently, a good deal into society," said Clara timidly. "Society will come back to town very soon now—at least, some of it."

"Oh, yes, I dare say. Society! No, thank you, with company manners. I want to laugh, and talk, and enjoy myself."

The champagne, in fact, had made her forget the instructions of her tutor. At all events, she looked anything but "quiet," with her face flushed and her eyes bright. Suddenly she caught Arnold's expression of suspicion and watchfulness, and resolutely subdued a rising inclination to get up from the table and have a walk round with a snatch of a Topical Song.

"Forgive me, Clara," she murmured in her sweetest tone, "forgive me, cousin. I feel as if I must break out a bit, now and then. Yankee manners, you know. Let me stay quiet with you for a while. You know the thought of starched and stiff London society quite frightens me. I am not used to anything stiff. Let me stay at home quiet, with you."

"Dear girl!" cried Clara, her eyes filling with tears; "she has all Claude's affectionate softness of heart."

"I believe," said Arnold, later on in the evening, "that she must have been a circus rider, or something of that sort. What on earth does Clara mean by the gentle blood breaking out? We nearly had a breaking out at dinner, but it certainly was not due to the gentle blood."

After dinner, Arnold found her sitting on a sofa with Clara, who was telling her something about the glories of the Deseret family. He was half inclined to pity the girl, or to laugh—he was not certain which—for the patience with which she listened, in order to make amends for any bad impression she might have produced at dinner. He asked her, presently, if she would play. She might be, and certainly was, vulgar; but she could play well and she knew good music. People generally think that good music softens manners, and does not permit those who play and practice it to be vulgar. But, concerning this young person, so much could not be said with any truth.

"You play very well. Where did you learn? Who was your master?" Arnold asked.

She began to reply, but stopped short. He had very nearly caught her.

"Don't ask questions," she said. "I told you not to ask questions before. Where should I learn, but in America? Do you suppose no one can play the piano, except in England? Look here," she glanced at her cousin. "Do you, Mr. Arbuthnot, always spend your evenings like this?"

"How like this?"

"Why, going around in a swallow tail to drawing-rooms with the women, like a tame tom-cat. If you do, you must be a truly good young man. If you don't, what do you do?"

"Very often I spend my evenings in a drawing-room."

"Oh, Lord! Do most young Englishmen carry on in the same proper way?"

"Why not?"

"Don't they go to music-halls, please, and dancing cribs, and such?"

"Perhaps. But what does it concern us to know what some men do?"

"Oh, not much. Only if I were a man like you, I wouldn't consent to be a tame tom-cat—that is all; but perhaps you like it."

She meant to insult and offend him so that he should not

come any more.

But she did not succeed. He only laughed, feeling that he was getting below the surface, and sat down beside the piano.

"You amuse me," he said, "and you astonish me. You are, in fact, the most astonishing person I ever met. For instance, you come from America, and you talk pure London slang with a cockney twang. How did it get there?"

In fact, it was not exactly London slang, but a patois or dialect, learned partly from her husband, partly from her companions, and partly brought from Gloucester.

"I don't know—I never asked. It came wrapped up in brown paper, perhaps, with a string round it."

"You have lived in America all your life, and you look more like an Englishwoman than any other girl I have ever seen."

"Do I? So much the better for the English girls; they can't do better than take after me. But perhaps—most likely, in fact— you think that American girls all squint, perhaps, or have got humpbacks? Anything else?"

"You were brought up in a little American village, and yet you play in the style of a girl who has had the best masters."

She did not explain—it was not necessary to explain—that her master had been her father who was a teacher of music.

"I can't help it, can I?" she asked; "I can't help it if I turned out different to what you expected. People sometimes do, you know. And when you don't approve of a girl, it's English manners, I suppose, to tell her so—kind of encourages her to persevere, and pray for better luck next time, doesn't it? It's simple too, and prevents any foolish errors—no mistake afterward, you see. I say, are you going to come here often; because, if you are, I shall go away back to the States or somewhere, or stay upstairs in my own room. You and me won't get on very well together, I am afraid."

"I don't think you will see me very often," he replied. "That is improbable; yet I dare say I shall come here as often as I usually do."

"What do you mean by that?" She looked sharply and suspiciously at him. He repeated his words, and she perceived that there was meaning in them, and she felt uneasy.

"I don't understand at all," she said; "Clara tells me that this house is mine. Now—don't you know—I don't intend to invite any but my own friends to visit me in my own house?"

"That seems reasonable. No one can expect you to invite people who are not your friends."

"Well, then, I ain't likely to call you my friend"—Arnold inclined his head—"and I am not going to talk riddles any more. Is there anything else you want to say?"

"Nothing more, I think, at present, thank you."

"If there is, you know, don't mind me—have it out—I'm nobody, of course. I'm not expected to have any manners— I'm only a girl. You can say what you please to me, and be as rude as you please; Englishmen always are as rude as they can be to American girls—I've always heard that."

Arnold laughed.

"At all events," he said, "you have charmed Clara, which is the only really important thing. Good-night, Miss—Miss Deseret."

"Good-night, old man," she said, laughing, because she bore no malice, and had given him a candid opinion; "I dare say when you get rid of your fine company manners, and put off your swallow tail, you're not a bad sort, after all. Perhaps, if you would confess, you are as fond of a kick-up on your way home as anybody. Trust you quiet chaps!"

Clara had not fortunately heard much of this conversation, which, indeed, was not meant for her, because the girl was playing all the time some waltz music, which enabled her to talk and play without being heard at the other end of the room.

*   *   *   *   *

Well, there was now no doubt. The American physician and the subject of the photograph were certainly the same man. And this man was also the thief of the safe, and Iris Aglen was Iris Deseret. Of that, Arnold had no longer any reasonable doubt. There was, however, one thing more. Before leaving Clara's house, he refreshed his memory as to the Deseret arms. The quarterings of the shield were, so far, exactly what Mr. Emblem recollected.

"It is," said Lala Roy, "what I thought. But, as yet, not a word to Iris."

He then proceeded to relate the repentance, the confession, and the atonement proposed by the remorseful James. But he did not tell quite all. For the wise man never tells all. What really happened was this. When James had made a clean breast and confessed his enormous share in the villainy, Lala Roy bound him over to secrecy under pain of Law, Law the Rigorous, pointing out that although they do not, in England, exhibit the Kourbash, or bastinado the soles of the feet, they make the prisoner sleep on a hard board, starve him on skilly, set him to work which tears his nails from his fingers, keep him from conversation, tobacco, and drink, and when he comes out, so hedge him around with prejudice and so clothe him with a robe of shame, that no one will ever employ him again, and he is therefore doomed to go back again to the English Hell. Lala Roy, though a man of few words, drew so vivid a description of the punishment which awaited his penitent that James, foxy as he was by nature, felt constrained to resolve that henceforth, happen what might, then and for all future, he would range himself on the side of virtue, and as a beginning he promised to do everything that he could for the confounding of Joseph and the bringing of the guilty to justice.

CHAPTER XIII

HIS LAST CHANCE

Three days elapsed, during which nothing was done. That cause is strongest which can afford to wait. But in those three days several things happened.

First of all, Mr. David Chalker, seeing that the old man was obdurate, made up his mind to lose most of his money, and cursed Joe continually for having led him to build upon his grandfather's supposed wealth. Yet he ought to have known. Tradesmen do not lock up their savings in investments for their grandchildren, nor do they borrow small sums at ruinous interest of money-lending solicitors; nor do they give Bills of Sale. These general rules were probably known to Mr. Chalker. Yet he did not apply them to this particular case. The neglect of the General Rule, in fact, may lead the most astute of mankind into ways of foolishness.

James, for his part, stimulated perpetually by fear of prison and loss of character and of situation—for who would employ an assistant who got keys made to open the safe?—showed himself the most repentant of mortals. Dr. Joseph Washington, lulled into the most perfect security, enjoyed all those pleasures which the sum of three hundred pounds could purchase. Nobody knew where he was, or what he was doing. As for Lotty, she had established herself firmly in Chester Square, and Cousin Clara daily found out new and additional proofs of the gentle blood breaking out!

Walter Besant

On the fourth morning Lala Roy sallied forth. He was about to make a great Moral Experiment, the nature of which you will immediately understand. None but a philosopher who had studied Confucius and Lao Kiun, would have conceived so fine a scheme.

First he paid a visit to Mr. Chalker.

The office was the ground-floor front room, in one of the small streets north of the King's Road. It was not an imposing office, nor did it seem as if much business was done there; and one clerk of tender years sufficed for Mr. Chalker's wants.

"Oh!" he said, "it's our friend from India. You're a lodger of old Emblem's, ain't you?"

"I have lived with him for twenty years. I am his friend."

"Very well. I dare say we shall come to terms, if he's come to his senses. Just take a chair and sit down. How is the old man?"

"He has not yet recovered the use of his intellect."

"Oh! Then how can you act for him if he's off his head?"

"I came to ask an English creditor to show mercy."

"Mercy? What is the man talking about? Mercy! I want my money. What has that got to do with mercy?"

"Nothing, truly; but I will give you your money. I will give you justice, and you shall give me mercy. You lent Mr. Emblem fifty pounds. Will you take your fifty pounds, and leave us in peace?"

He drew a bag out of his pocket—a brown banker's bag—and Mr. Chalker distinctly heard the rustling of notes.

This is a sound which to some ears is more delightful than the finest music in the world. It awakens all the most pleasurable emotions; it provokes desire and hankering after possession; and it fills the soul with the imaginary enjoyment of wealth.

"Certainly not," said Mr. Chalker, confident that better terms than those would be offered. "If that is all you have to say, you may go away again."

"But the rest is usury. Think! To give fifty, and ask three hundred and fifty, is the part of an usurer."

"Call it what you please. The bill of sale is for three hundred and fifty pounds. Pay that three hundred and fifty, with costs and sheriff's poundage, and I take away my man. If you don't pay it, then the books on the shelves and the furniture of the house go to the hammer."

"The books, I am informed," said Lala Roy, "will not bring as much as a hundred pounds if they are sold at auction. As for the furniture, some of it is mine, and some belongs to Mr. Emblem's granddaughter."

"His granddaughter! Oh, it's a swindle," said Mr. Chalker angrily. "It is nothing more or less than a rank swindle. The old man ought to be prosecuted, and, mind you, I'll prosecute him, and you too, for conspiring with him."

"A prosecution," said the Hindoo, "will not hurt him, but it might hurt you. For it would show how you lent him fifty pounds five years ago; how you made him give you a bill for a hundred; how you did not press him to pay that bill, but you continually offered to renew it for him, increasing the amount on each time of renewal; and at last you made him give you a bill of sale for three hundred and fifty. This is, I suppose, one of the many ways in which Englishmen grow rich. There are also usurers in India, but they do not, in my country, call themselves lawyers. A prosecution. My friend, it is for us to prosecute. Shall we show that you have done the same thing with many others? You are, by this time, well known in the neighborhood, Mr. Chalker, and you are so much beloved that there are many who would be delighted to relate their experiences and dealings with so clever a man. Have you ever studied, one asks with wonder, the Precepts of the great Sage who founded your religion?"

"Oh, come, don't let us have any religious nonsense!"

"I assure you they are worth studying. I am, myself, an humble follower of Gautama, but I have read those precepts with profit. In the kingdom imagined by that preacher, there is no room for usurers, Mr. Chalker. Where, then, will be your kingdom? Every man must be somewhere. You must have a kingdom and a king."

"This is tomfoolery!" Mr. Chalker turned red, and looked very uncomfortable. "Stick to business. Payment in full. Those are my terms."

"You think, then, that the Precepts of your Sage are only intended for men while they sit in the church? Many Englishmen think so, I have observed."

"Payment in full, mister. That's what I want."

He banged his fist on the table.

"No abatement? No mercy shown to an old man on the edge of the grave? Think, Mr. Chalker. You will soon be as old as Mr. Emblem, your hair as white, your reason as unsteady—"

"Payment in full, and no more words."

"It is well. Then, Mr. Chalker, I have another proposal to make to you."

"I thought we should come to something more. Out with it!"

"I believe you are a friend of Mr. Emblem's grandson?"

"Joe? Oh yes, I know Joe."

"You know him intimately?"

"Yes, I may say so."

"You know that he forged his grandfather's name; that he is a profligate and a spendthrift, and that he has taken or borrowed from his grandfather whatever money he could get, and that—in short, he is a friend of your own?"

It was not until after his visitor had gone that Mr. Chalker understood, and began to resent this last observation.

"Go on," he said. "I know all about Joe."

"Good. Then, if you can tell me anything about him which may be of use to me I will do this. I will pay you double the valuation of Mr. Emblem's shop, in return, for a receipt in full. If you can not, you may proceed to sell everything by auction."

Mr. Chalker hesitated. A valuation would certainly give a higher figure than a forced sale, and then that valuation doubled!

"Well," he said, "I don't know. It's a cruel hard case to be done out of my money. How am I to find out whether anything I tell you would be of use to you or not? What kind of thing do you want? How do I know that if you get what you want, you won't swear it is of no use to you?"

"You have the word of one who never broke his word."

Mr. Chalker laughed derisively.

"Why," he said, "I wouldn't take the word of an English bishop—no, nor of an archbishop—where money is concerned. What is it—what is the kind of thing you want to know?"

"It is concerned with a certain woman."

"Oh, well, if it is only a woman! I thought it might be something about money. Joe, you see, like a good many other people, has got his own ideas about money, and perhaps he isn't so strict in his dealings as he might be—few men are—and I should not like to let out one or two things that only him and me know." In fact, Mr. Chalker saw, in imagination, the burly form of Joe in his office, brandishing a stick, and accusing him of friendship's trust betrayed.

"But as it is only a woman—which of 'em is it?"

"This is a young woman, said to be handsome, tall, and finely-made; she has, I am told, light brown hair and large eyes. That is the description of her given to me."

"I know the girl you mean. Splendid figure, and goes well in tights?"

"I have not been informed on that subject. Can you tell me any more about her?"

"I suspect, mister," said Joe's friend, with cunning eyes, "that you've made the acquaintance of a certain widow that was—married woman that is. I remember now, I've seen Hindoos about her lodgings, down Shadwell way."

"Perhaps," said Lala, "and perhaps not." His face showed not the least sign which could be read. "You can tell me afterward what you know of the woman at Shadwell."

"Well, then, Joe thinks I know nothing about it. Else I wouldn't tell you. Because I don't want a fight with Joe. Is this any use to you? He is married to the girl as well as to the widow."

"He is married to the girl as well as to the widow. He has, then, two wives. It is against the English custom, and breaks the English law. The young wife who is beautiful, and the old wife who has the lodging-house. Very good. What is the address of this woman?"

Mr. Chalker looked puzzled.

"Don't you know it, then? What are you driving at?"

"What is the name and address of this Shadwell woman?"

"Well, then"—he wrote an address and handed it over—"you may be as close as you like. I don't care. It isn't my business. But you won't make me believe you don't know all about her. Look here, whatever happens, don't say I told you."

"It shall be a secret," said Lala, taking out the bag of notes. "Let us complete the business at once, Mr. Chalker. Here is another offer. I will give you two hundred pounds in discharge of your whole claim, or you shall have a valuation made, if you prefer it, and I will double the amount."

Mr. Chalker chose the former promptly, and in a few moments handed over the necessary receipts, and sent his clerk to recall the Man in Possession.

"What are you going to do with Joe?" he asked. "No good turn, I'll swear. And a more unforgiving face than yours I never set eyes on. It isn't my business, but I'll give you one warning. If you make Joe desperate, he'll turn on you; and Lord help your slender ribs if Joe once begins. Don't make him desperate. And now I'll tell you another thing. First, the woman at Shadwell is horribly jealous. She'll make a row. Next, the young one, who sings at a music-hall, she's desperately in love with her husband—more than he is with her—and if a woman's in love with a man, there's one thing she never forgives. You understand what that is. Between the pair, Joe's likely to have a rough time."

"I do. I have had many wives myself."

"Oh, Lord, he says he's had many wives! How many?"

Lala Roy read the receipt, and put it in his pocket. Then he rose and remarked, with a smile of supreme superiority:

"It is a pleasure to give money to you, and to such as you, Mr. Chalker."

"Is it?" he replied with a grin. "Give me some more, then."

"You are one of those who, the richer they become, the less harm they do. Many Englishmen are of this disposition. When they are poor they are jackals, hyenas, wolves, and man-eating tigers; when they are rich they are benevolent and charitable, and show mercy unto the wretched and the poor. So that, in their case, the words of the Wise Man are naught, when he says that the earth is barren of good things where she hoardeth treasure; and that where gold is in her bowels no herb groweth. Pray, Mr. Chalker, pray earnestly for gold in order that you may become virtuous."

Mr. Chalker grinned, but looked uncomfortable.

"I will, mister," he said, "I will pray with all my might."

Nevertheless, he remained for the space of the whole morning in uneasiness. The words of the Philosopher troubled him. I do not go so far as to say that his mind went back to the days when he was young and innocent, because he was still young, and he never had been innocent; nor do I say that a tear rose to his eyes and trickled down his cheek, because nothing brought tears into his eyes except a speck of dust; or that he resolved to confine himself for the future to legitimate lawyer's work, because he would then have starved. I only say that he felt uncomfortable and humiliated, and chiefly so because an old man with white hair and a brown skin—hang it! a common nigger—had been able to bring discord into the sweet harmony of his thoughts.

Lala Roy then betook himself to Joe's former lodgings, and asked for that gentleman's present address.

The landlady professed to know nothing.

"You do know, however," he persisted, reading knowledge in her eyes.

"Is it trouble you mean for him?" asked the woman, "and him such a fine, well-set-up young man, too! Is it trouble? Oh, dear, I always thought he got his money on the cross. Look here. I ain't going to round on him, though he has gone away and left a comfortable room. So there! And you may go."

Lala Roy opened his hand. There were at least five golden sovereigns glorifying his dingy palm.

"Can gold," the moralist asked, "ever increase the virtue of man? Woman, how much?"

"Is it trouble?" she repeated, looking greedily at the money. "Will the young man get copped?"

Lala understood no London slang. But he showed his hand again.

"How much? Who so is covetous let him know that his heart is poor. How much?"

"Poor young man! I'll take them all, please, sir. What's he done?"

"Where does he live?"

"I know where he lives," she said, "because our Bill rode away with him at the back of his cab, and saw where he got out. He's married now, and his wife sings at the music-hall, and he lives on her earnings. Quite the gentleman he is now, and smokes cigars all day long. There's his address, and thank you for the money. Oh," she said with a gasp. "To think that people can earn five pounds so easy."

"May the gold procure you happiness—such happiness as you desire!" said Lala Roy.

"It will nearly pay the quarter's rent. And that's about happiness enough for one morning."

Joe was sitting in his room alone, half asleep. In fact, he had a head upon him. He sprung to his feet, however, when he saw Lala Roy.

"Hallo!" he cried. "You here, Nig? How the devil did you find out my address?"

There was not only astonishment, but some alarm upon his countenance.

"Never mind. I want a little conversation with you, Mr. Joseph."

"Well, sit down and let us have it out. I say, have you come to tell me that you did sneak those papers, after all? What did you get for them?"

"I have not come to tell you that. I dare say, however, we shall be able, some day, to tell you who did steal the papers—if any were stolen, that is."

"Quite so, my jolly mariner. If any were stolen. Ho, ho! you've got to prove that first, haven't you? How's the old man?"

"He is ill; he is feeble with age; he is weighed down with misfortune. I am come, Mr. Joseph, to ask your help for him."

"My help for him? Why, can't he help himself?"

"Four or five years ago he incurred a debt for one who forged his name. He needed not to have paid that money, but he saved a man from prison."

"Who was that? Who forged his name?"

"I do not name that man, whose end will be confusion, unless he repent and make amends. This debt has grown until it is too large for him to pay it. Unless it is paid, his whole property, his very means of living, will be sold by the creditor."

"How can I pay him back? It is three hundred and fifty pounds now," said Joseph.

"Man, thou hast named thyself."

Joseph stammered but blustered still.

"Well—then—what the devil do you mean—you and your forgery?"

"Forgery is one crime: you have since committed, perhaps, others. Think. You have been saved once from prison. Will any one save you a second time? How have you shown your gratitude? Will you now do something for your benefactor?"

"What do you mean, I say? What do you mean by your forgery and prison? Hang me, if I oughtn't to kick you out of the room. I would, too, if you were ten years younger. Do you know, sir, that you are addressing an officer and a gentleman?"

"There is sometimes, even at the very end, a door opened for repentance. The door is open now. Young man, once more, consider. Your grandfather is old and destitute. Will you help him?"

Joseph hesitated.

"I don't believe he is poor. He has saved up all his money for the girl; let her help him."

"You are wrong. He has saved nothing. His granddaughter maintains herself by teaching. He has not a penny. You have got from him, and you have spent all the money he had."

"He ought to have saved."

"He could, at least, have lived by his calling but for you and for this debt which was incurred by you. He is ruined by it. What will you do for him?"

"I am not going to do anything for him," said Joseph. "Is it likely? Did he ever have anything but a scowl for me?"

"He who injures another is always in the wrong. You will, then, do nothing? Think. It is the open door. He is your grandfather; he has kept you from starvation when you were turned out of office for drink and dishonesty. I heard that you now have money. I have been told that you have been seen to show a large sum of money. Will you give him some?"

As a matter of fact, Joe had been, the night before, having a festive evening at the music-hall, from which his wife was absent, owing to temporary indisposition. While there, he took so much Scotch whisky and water that his tongue was loosened and he became boastful; and that to so foolish an extent that he actually brandished in the eyes of the multitude a whole handful of banknotes. He now remembered this, and was greatly struck by the curious fact that Lala Roy should seem to know it.

"I haven't got any money. It was all brag last night. I couldn't help my grandfather if I wanted to."

"You have what is left of three hundred pounds," said Lala Roy.

"If I said that last night," replied Joe, "I must have been

drunker than I thought. You old fool! the flimsies were duffers. Where do you think I could raise three hundred pounds? No, no—I'm sorry for the old man, but I can't help him. I'm going to see him again in a day or two. We jolly sailors don't make much money, but if a pound or two, when I come home, will be of any use to him, he's only got to say the word. After all, I believe it's a kid, got up between you. The old man must have saved something."

"You will suffer him, then, even to be taken to the workhouse?"

"Why, I can't help it, and I suppose you'll have to go there too. Ho, ho! I say, Nig!" He began to laugh. "Ho, ho! They won't let you wear that old fez of yours at the workhouse. How beautiful you'll look in the workhouse uniform, won't you? I'll come home, and bring you some 'baccy. Now you can cheese it, old 'un."

"I will go, if that is what you mean. It is the last time that you will be asked to help your grandfather. The door is closed. You have had one more chance, and you have thrown it away."

So he departed, and Joe, who was of a self-reliant and sanguine disposition, thought nothing of the warning, which was therefore thrown away and wasted.

As for Lala, he called a cab, and drove to Shadwell. And if any man ever felt that he was an instrument set apart to carry out a scheme of vengeance, that Hindoo philosopher felt like one. The Count of Monte Cristo himself was not more filled with the faith and conviction of his divine obligation.

In the afternoon he returned to Chelsea, and perhaps one who knew him might have remarked upon his face something like a gleam of satisfaction. He had done his duty.

It was now five days since the fatal discovery. Mr. Emblem still remained upstairs in his chair; but he was slowly recovering.

He clearly remembered that he had been robbed, and the principal sign of the shock was his firm conviction that by his own exercise of memory Iris had been enabled to enter into possession of her own.

As regards the Bill of Sale, he had clean forgotten it. Now, in the morning, there happened a thing which surprised James very much. The Man in Possession was recalled. He went away. So that the money must have been paid. James was so astonished that he ran upstairs to tell Iris.

"Then," said the girl, "we shall not be turned out after all. But who has paid the money?"

It could have been no other than Arnold. Yet when, later in the day, he was taxed with having committed the good action, Arnold stoutly denied it. He had not so much money in the world, he said; in fact, he had no money at all.

"The good man," said the Philosopher, "has friends of whom he knoweth not. As the river returns its waters to the sea, so the heart rejoiceth in returning benefits received."

"Oh, Lala," said Iris. "But on whom have we conferred any benefits?"

"The moon shines upon all alike," said Lala, "and knows not what she illumines."

"Lala Roy," said Arnold, suddenly getting a gleam of intelligence, "it is you who have paid this money."

"You, Lala?"

"No one else could have paid it," said Arnold.

"But I thought—I thought—" said Iris.

"You thought I had no money at all. Children, I have some.

One may live without money in Hindostan, but in England even the Philosopher cannot meditate unless he can pay for food and shelter. I have money, Iris, and I have paid the usurer enough to satisfy him. Let us say no more."

"Oh, Lala!" The tears came to Iris's eyes. "And now we shall go on living as before."

"I think not," he replied. "In the generations of Man, the seasons continue side by side; but spring does not always continue with winter."

"I know, now," interrupted Mr. Emblem, suddenly waking into life and recollection; "I could not remember at first. Now I know very well, but I cannot tell how, that the man who stole my papers is my own grandson. James would not steal. James is curious; he wants to read over my shoulders what I am writing. He would pry and find out. But he would not steal. It doesn't matter much—does it?—since I was able to repair the loss—I always had a most excellent memory—and Iris has now received her inheritance; but it is my grandson Joe who has stolen the papers. My daughter's son came home from Australia when—but this I learned afterward—he had already disgraced himself there. He ran into debt, and I paid his debts; he forged my name and I accepted the bill; he took all the money I could let him have, and still he asked for more. There is no one in the world who would rob me of those papers except Joseph."

Now, the door was open to the staircase, and the door of communication between the shop and the house-passage was also open. This seems a detail hardly worth noting; yet it proved of the greatest importance. From such small trifles follow great events. Observe that as yet no positive proof was in the hands of the two conspirators which would actually connect Iris with Claude Deseret. The proofs were in the stolen papers, and though Clara had those papers, who was to show that these papers were actually those in the sealed packet?

When Mr. Emblem finished speaking, no one replied, because Arnold and Lala knew the facts already, but did not wish to spread them abroad: and next, because to Iris it was nothing new that her cousin was a bad man, and because she thought, now that the Man in Possession was gone, they might just as well forget the papers, and go on as if all this fuss had not happened.

In the silence that followed this speech, they heard the voice of James down-stairs, saying:

"I am sorry to say, sir, that Mr. Emblem is ill upstairs, and you can't see him to-day."

"Ill, is he? I am very sorry. Take him my compliments, James. Mr. Frank Farrar's compliments, and tell him—"

And then Mr. Emblem sprung to his feet, crying:

"Stop him! stop him! Go down-stairs, some one, and stop him! I don't know where he lives. Stop him! stop him!"

Arnold rushed down the stairs. He found in the shop an elderly gentleman, carrying a bundle of books. It was, in fact, Mr. Farrar come to negotiate the sale of another work from his library.

"I beg your pardon, sir," said Arnold, "Mr. Emblem is most anxious to see you. Would you step upstairs?"

"Quick, Mr. Farrar—quick," the old man held him tight by the hand. "Tell me before my memory runs away with me again—tell me. Listen, Iris! Yet it doesn't matter, because you have already—Tell me—" He seemed about to wander again, but he pulled himself together with a great effort. "You knew my son-in-law before his marriage?"

"Surely, Mr. Emblem; I knew your son-in-law, and his father, and all his people."

"And his name was not Aglen, at all?" asked Arnold.

"No; he took the name of Aglen from a fancied feeling of pride when he quarreled with his father about—well, it was about his marriage, as you know, Mr. Emblem; he came to London, and tried to make his way by writing, and thought to do it, and either to hide a failure or brighten a success, by using a pseudonym. People were more jealous about their names in those days. He had better," added the unsuccessful veteran of letters, "he had far better have made his living as a—as a"—he looked about him for a fitting simile—"as a bookseller."

"Then, sir," said Arnold, "what was his real name?"

"His name was Claude Deseret, of course."

"Iris," said Arnold, taking her hand, "this is the last proof. We have known it for four or five days, but we wanted the final proof, and now we have it. My dear, you are the cousin of Clara Holland, and all her fortune, by her grandfather's will, is yours. This is the secret of the safe. This was what the stolen papers told you."

CHAPTER XIV

THE HAND OF FATE

At the first stroke of noon next day, Arnold arrived at his cousin's house in Chester Square. He was accompanied by Iris, by Lala Roy, and by Mr. Frank Farrar.

"Pray, Arnold, what is meant by all this mystery?" asked Clara, receiving him and his party with considerable surprise.

"I will explain all in a few minutes, my dear Clara. Meanwhile, have you done what you promised?"

"Yes, I wrote to Dr. Washington. He will be here, I expect, in a few minutes."

"You wrote exactly in the form of words you promised me?"

"Yes, exactly. I asked him to meet me here this morning at a quarter past twelve, in order to discuss a few points connected with Iris's future arrangements, before he left for America, and I wrote on the envelope, 'Immediate and important.'"

"Very well. He will be sure to come, I think. Perhaps your cousin will insist upon another check for fifty pounds being given to him."

"Arnold, you are extremely suspicious and most ungenerous about Dr. Washington, on whose truth and disinterested honesty I thoroughly rely."

"We shall see. Meanwhile, Clara, I desire to present to you a young lady of whom we have already spoken. This is Miss Aglen, who is, I need hardly say, deeply anxious to win your good opinion. And this is Lala Roy, an Indian gentleman who knew her father, and has lived in the same house with her for twenty years. Our debt—I shall soon be able to say your debt—of gratitude to this gentleman for his long kindness to Miss Aglen—is one which can never be repaid."

Clara gave the most frigid bow to both Iris and Lala Roy.

"Really, Arnold, you are talking in enigmas this morning. What am I to understand? What has this gentleman to do with my appointment with Dr. Washington?"

"My dear cousin, I am so happy this morning that I wonder I do not talk in conundrums, or rondeaux, or terza rima. It is a mere chance, I assure you. Perhaps I may break out in rhymes presently. This evening we will have fireworks in the square, roast a whole ox, invite the neighbors, and dance about a maypole. You shall lead off the dance, Clara."

"Pray go on, Arnold. All this is very inexplicable."

"This gentleman, however, is a very old friend of yours, Clara. Do you not recognize Mr. Frank Farrar, who used to stay at the Hall in the old days?

"I remember Mr. Farrar very well." Clara gave him her hand. "But I should not have known him. Why have we never met in society during all these years, Mr. Farrar?"

"I suppose because I have been out of society, Miss Holland," said the scholar. "When a man marries, and has a large family, and a small income, and grows old, and has to see the young fellows shoving him out at every point, he doesn't care much about society. I hope you are well and happy."

"I am very well, and I ought to be happy, because I have recovered Claude's lost heiress, my cousin, Iris Deseret, and she is the best and most delightful of girls, with the warmest heart and the sweetest instincts of a lady by descent and birth."

She looked severely at Arnold, who said nothing, but smiled incredulously.

Mr. Farrar looked from Iris to Miss Holland, bewildered.

"And why do you come to see me to-day, Mr. Farrar—and with Arnold?"

"Because I have undertaken to answer one question presently, which Mr. Arbuthnot is to ask me. That is why I am here. Not but what it gives me the greatest pleasure to see you again, Miss Holland, after so many years."

"Our poor Claude died in America, you know, Mr. Farrar."

"So I have recently heard."

"And left one daughter."

"That also I have learned." He looked at Iris.

"She is with me, here in this house, and has been with me for a week. You may understand, Mr. Farrar, the happiness I feel in having with me Claude's only daughter."

Mr. Farrar looked from her to Arnold with increasing amazement. But he said nothing.

"I have appointed this morning, at Arnold's request," Clara went on, "to have an interview, perhaps the last, with the gentleman who brought my dear Iris from America. I say, at Arnold's request, because he asked me to do this, and I have always trusted him implicitly, and I hope he is not going to bring trouble upon us now, although I do not, I confess, understand the presence of his friends or their connection with my cousin."

"My dear Clara," said Arnold again, "I ask for nothing but patience. And that only for a few moments. As for the papers, you have them all in your possession?"

"Yes; they are locked up in my strong-box."

"Do not, on any account, give them to anybody. However, after this morning you will not be asked. Have you taken as yet any steps at all for the transference of your property to—to the rightful heir?"

"Not yet."

"Thank goodness! And now, Clara, I will ask you, as soon as Dr. Washington and—your cousin—are in the drawing-room, to ring the bell. You need not explain why. We will answer the summons, and we will give all the explanations that may be required."

"I will not have my cousin vexed, Arnold."

"You shall not. Your cousin shall never be vexed by me as long as I live."

"And Dr. Washington must not be in any way offended. Consider the feelings of an American gentleman, Arnold. He is my guest."

"You may thoroughly rely upon my consideration for the feelings of an American gentleman. Go; there is a knock at the door. Go to receive him, and, when both are in the room, ring the bell."

Joe was in excellent spirits that morning. His interview with Lala Roy convinced him that nothing whatever was known of the papers, therefore nothing could be suspected. What a fool, he thought, must be his grandfather, to have had these papers in his hands for eighteen years and never to have opened the packet, in obedience to the injunction of a dead man! Had it been his own case, he would have opened the papers without the least delay, mastered the contents, and instantly claimed the property. He would have gone on to use it for his own purposes and private gain, and with an uninterrupted run of eighteen years, he would most certainly have made a very pretty thing out of it.

However, everything works well for him who greatly dares. His wife would manage for him better than he could do it for himself. Yet a few weeks, and the great fortune would fall into his hands. He walked all the way to Chester Square, considering how he should spend the money. There are some forms of foolishness, such as, say, those connected with art, literature, charity, and work for others, which attract some rich men, but which he was not at all tempted to commit. There were others, however, connected with horses, races, betting, and gambling, which tempted him strongly. In fact, Joseph contemplated spending this money wholly on his own pleasures. Probably it would be a part of his pleasure to toss a few crumbs to his wife.

It is sad to record that Lotty, finding herself received with so much enthusiasm, had already begun to fall off in her behavior. Even Clara, who thought she discovered every hour some new point of resemblance in the girl to her father, was fain to admit that the "Americanisms" were much too pronounced for general society.

Her laugh was louder and more frequent; her jests were rough and common; she used slang words freely; her gestures were extravagant, and she walked in the streets as if she wished every one to notice her. It is the walk of the Music-Hall stage, and the trick of it consists chiefly in giving, so to speak, prominence to the shoulders and oscillation to the skirts. In fact, she was one of those ladies who ardently desire that all the world should notice them.

Further, in her conversation, she showed an acquaintance with certain phases of the English lower life which was astonishing in an American girl. But Clara had no suspicion—none whatever. One thing the girl did which pleased her mightily.

She was never tired of hearing about her father, and his way of looking, standing, walking, folding his hands, and holding himself. And constantly more and more Clara detected these little tricks in his daughter. Perhaps she learned them.

"My dear," she said, "to think that I ever thought you unlike your dear father!"

So that it made her extremely uncomfortable to detect a certain reserve in Arnold toward the girl, and then a dislike of Arnold in the girl herself. However, she was accustomed to act by Arnold's advice, and consented, when he asked her, to arrange so that Arnold might meet Dr. Washington. As if anything that so much as looked like suspicion could be thought of for a moment!

But the bell rang, and Arnold, followed by his party, led the way from the morning room to the drawing room. Dr. Joseph Washington was standing with his back to the door. The girl was dressed as if she had just come from a walk, and was holding Clara's hand.

"Yes, madam," he was saying softly, "I return to-morrow to America, and my wife and my children. I leave our dear girl in the greatest confidence in your hands. I only venture to advise that, to avoid lawyers' expenses, you should simply instruct somebody—the right person—to transfer the property from your name to the name of Iris. Then you will be saved troubles and formalities of every kind. As for me, my home is in America—"

"No, Joseph," said Lala Roy gently; "it is in Shadwell."

"It is a lie!" he cried, starting; "it is an infernal lie!"

"Iris," said Arnold, "lift your veil, my dear. Mr. Farrar, who is this young lady? Look upon this face, Clara."

"This is the daughter of Claude Deseret," said Mr. Farrar, "if she is the daughter of the man who married Alice Emblem, and went by the name of Aglen."

Clara turned a terrified face to Arnold.

"Arnold, help me!"

"Whose face is this?" he repeated.

"It is—good Heavens!—it is the face of your portrait. It is Claude's face again. They are his very eyes—" She covered her face with her hands. "Oh, Arnold, what is it! Who is this other?"

"This other lady, Clara, is a Music-Hall Singer, who calls herself Carlotta Claridane, wife of this man, who is not an American at all, but the grandson of Mr. Emblem, the bookseller, and therefore cousin of Iris. It is he who robbed his grandfather of the papers which you have in your possession, Clara. And this is an audacious conspiracy, which we have been so fortunate as to unearth and detect, step by step."

"Oh, can such wickedness be?" said Clara; "and in my house, too?"

"Joe," said Lotty, "the game is up. I knew it wouldn't last."

"Let them prove it," said Joe; "let them prove it. I defy you to prove it."

"Don't be a fool, Joe," said his wife. "Remember," she whispered, "you've got a pocketful of money. Let us go peaceably."

"As for you, Nigger," said Joe, "I'll break every bone in your body."

"Not here," said Arnold; "there will be no breaking of bones in this house."

Lotty began to laugh.

"The gentle blood always shows itself, doesn't it?" she said. "I've got the real instincts of a lady, haven't I? Oh, it was beautiful while it lasted. And every day more and more like my father."

"Arnold," cried poor Clara, crushed, "help me!"

"Come," said Arnold, "you had better go at once."

"I won't laugh at you," said Lotty. "It's a shame, and you're a good old thing. But it did me good, it really did, to hear all about the gentle blood. Come, Joe. Let us go away quietly."

She took her husband's arm. Joe was standing sullen and desperate. Mr. Chalker was right. It wanted very little more to make him fall upon the whole party, and go off with a fight.

"Young woman," said Lala Roy, "you had better not go outside the house with the man. It will be well for you to wait until he has gone."

"Why? He is my husband, whatever we have done, and I'm not ashamed of him."

"Is he your husband? Ask him what I meant when I said his home was at Shadwell."

"Come, Lotty," said Joe, with a curious change of manner. "Let us go at once."

"Wait," Lala repeated. "Wait, young woman, let him go first. Pray—pray let him go first."

"Why should I wait? I go with my husband."

"I thought to save you from shame. But if you will go with him, ask him again why his home is at Shadwell, and why he left his wife."

Lotty sprung upon her husband, and caught his wrists with both hands.

"Joe, what does he mean? Tell me he is a liar."

"That would be useless," said Lala Roy. "Because a very few minutes will prove the contrary. Better, however, that he should go to prison for marrying two wives than for robbing his grandfather's safe."

"It's a lie!" Joe repeated, looking as dangerous as a wild boar brought to bay.

"There was a Joseph Gallop, formerly assistant purser in the service of the Peninsular and Oriental Steam Navigation Company," continued the man of fate, "who married, nine months ago, a certain widow at Shadwell. He was turned out of the service, and he married her because she had a prosperous lodging-house."

"Oh—h!" cried Lotty. "You villain! You thought to live upon my earnings, did you? You put me up to pretend to be somebody else. Miss Holland"—she fell upon her knees, literally and simply, and without any theatrical pretense at all—"forgive me! I am properly punished. Oh, he is made of lies! He told me that the real Iris was dead and buried, and he was the rightful heir; and as for you"—she sprung to her feet and turned upon her husband—"I know it is true. I know it is true—I can see it within your guilty eyes."

"If you have any doubt," said Lala, "here is a copy of the marriage-certificate."

She took it, read it, and put it in her pocket. Then she went out of the room without another word, but with rage and revenge in her eyes.

Joseph followed her, saying no more. He had lost more than he thought to lose. But there was still time to escape, and he had most of the money in his pocket.

But another surprise awaited him.

The lady from Shadwell, in fact, was waiting for him outside the door. With her were a few Shadwell friends, of the seafaring profession, come to see fair play. It was a disgraceful episode in the history of Chester Square. After five minutes or so, during which no welsher on a race-course was ever more hardly used, two policemen interfered to rescue the man of two wives, and there was a procession all the way to the police-court, where, after several charges of assault had been preferred and proved against half a dozen mariners, Joseph was himself charged with bigamy, both wives giving evidence, and committed for trial.

His old friend, Mr. David Chalker, one is sorry to add, refused to give bail, so that he remained in custody, and will now endure hardness for a somewhat lengthened period.

"Clara," said Arnold, "Iris will stay with you, if you ask her. We shall not marry, my dear, without your permission. I have promised that already, have I not?"

Walter Besant

CHAPTER XV

A YACHTSMAN'S YARN

"I've knocked off the sea now for some years, but I was yachting along with all sorts of gentlemen and in all sorts of craft, from three to one hundred and twenty tons, ever since the top of my head was no higher than your knee; and as boy, man, and master, I'll allow there's no one who has seen much more than I have. Yet, spite of that, I can recall but one extraordinary circumstance. Daresay when I've told it you, you won't believe it; but I sha'n't be able to help that. Truth's truth, no consequence how sing'lar its appearance may be; and so now to begin.

"No matter the port, no matter the yacht's name, no matter her owner's calling, no matter nothing. Terms and dates and the like shall be imaginary, and so let the vessel be a schooner of one hundred tons called the 'Evangeline,' and her owner Mr. Robinson, and me, who was captain of her, Jacob Williams. This'll furnish a creep you may go on sweeping with till Doomsday without raising what's dead and gone, though not forgotten, mind ye, from the bottom. Well, for a whole fortnight had the 'Evangeline' been moored in a snug berth alongside a pier wall. The English Channel was wide there, and it didn't need much sailing to find the Atlantic Ocean. I began to think all cruising was to come to an end; for Mr. Robinson was a man fond of keeping the sea, and I had never found a fortnight's lying by to his taste at all. But matters explained themselves after I'd seen him two or three times walking about with a very fine-looking female party. Mr. Robinson was a bachelor, his age I dare say about forty, with handsome whiskers, and one of those voices that show breeding in a man; ay, and the humblest ear that hears 'em recognizes them. I didn't take much notice of *her*, though I reckoned her large black eyes the beautifullest I had ever beheld in a female countenance. She seemed young—not more than eight-and-twenty—with what they call a fine figure, though, speaking for myself, I never had much opinion of small waists. Give me *bong poine*, as my old master, Sir Arthur Jones, used to say; and he ought to have known, for he had been studying female beauty for eighty year, and died, I reckon, of it.

"I considered it to be a case of courting, for she was a lady; there was no mistaking that; she held her head up like one, and dressed as real ladies do, expensively but plainly—ay, old Jacob knows; he didn't go yachting for years for nothing. But it wasn't for me to form opinions. My berth was an easy one— just a sprawl all day long with a pipe in my mouth, and a good night's rest to follow; and that was all it was my duty to think about.

"Well, one afternoon Mr. Robinson comes aboard alone, and says to me, 'Williams, at what hour will the tide serve to-morrow night?'

"Why, sir," says I, after thinking, "there'll be plenty of water at nine o'clock."

"Then," says he, 'see all ready, Williams, to get away to-morrow at that hour. We're off to—,' and he names a Mediterranean port.

"Right, sir," says I, though wondering a bit to myself, for the season was pretty well advanced, and I couldn't have guessed, from what I knew and had heard of him, that he would have pushed so far south.

"Well, at half past eight that evening the deck was hailed by a

Walter Besant

boat alongside, and up he comes handing a lady on board, thickly veiled, and they both went below as if they were in a hurry. Some parcels and a bit of a bandbox or so were chucked up to us by the watermen, who then shoved off. There was a nice little off-shore breeze a-blowing, and soon after nine we were clear of the harbor and sailing quietly along, the sea smooth and the moon rising red out of a smother of mist. Mr. Robinson came on deck and looked aloft to see what sail was made; I was at the tiller, and stepping up to me, he says—

"What d'yer think of the weather, Williams?"

"Why," says I, 'it seems as if it was going to keep fair.'

"There can't come too much wind for me," says he, 'short of a hurricane. Don't spare your cloths, let it blow as it may. You understand that?'

"Quite easily," says I.

"Now, this order I took to be as singular as our going to the Mediterranean, for Mr. Robinson was never a man to carry on; there was no racing in him; quiet sailing was his pleasure, and what his hurry was all of a sudden I couldn't imagine, though I guessed that the party in the cabin might have something to do with it. She came on deck after we had been under way about three quarters of an hour, this time without a veil, with what they call a turban hat on her head. There was plenty of moonlight, and I tell you that the very shadow she cast, and that lay like a carving of jet on ivory, looked beautiful on the white deck, so fine her figure was. Lord, how her big eyes flashed, too, when she drew my way and turned 'em to the moon! Being a sober, 'spectable man myself, with correct views on the bringing up of daughters, it seemed to be a queer start that if so be this young lady was keeping company with Mr. Robinson—being courted by him, you know—that her mother or some female connection wasn't along with her. P'raps they were married, I thought; might have been spliced that very morning. She had no gloves on, and whenever she walked with Mr. Robinson near to me, I'd take a long squint at her left hand; but there was no distinguishing a wedding-ring by moonshine, and even had it been broad daylight it would have been all the same, for the jewels lay so thick on her fingers you'd have fancied them sparkling with dew.

"Well, all that night it blew a soft, quiet wind, but for hours next day 'twas all dead calm, a light swell, the sunlight coming off the water hot as steam, and the yacht slewing round and round as if, like the rest of us, she was trying to find out where the wind meant to come from next. I never saw any man fret more over a calm than Mr. Robinson did over that. The lady didn't appear discomposed; she sat under the awning reading, and once when Mr. Robinson turned to look at her she ran her shining black eyes with a smiling roll around the sea, that was just the same as if she had said, 'Isn't it big enough?' for hang me if even I couldn't read the language in them sparklers of hers when she chose to lift the eyelashes off their meaning, unaccustomed as Jacob Williams ever was to female ways and the customs they pursue! But Mr. Robinson couldn't keep quiet. He kept on asking of me when I thought the wind was coming, and he was constantly getting up and staring round, and I'd notice he was always letting his cigar go out, which is a sure sign that either a man don't care about smoking, or else he's got something weighing upon his spirits. P'raps, thought I, it's stipulated that he's not to get married anywhere but in the port we're bound to, and that the license don't run so long as to allow for calms; but this I said to myself, with a wink at my own thoughts, for, though there's a good many things in this 'ere yearth that I don't understand, I must tell you Jacob Williams wasn't born without a mind.

"Well, time went on, and then a head-wind sprung up, with a short, spiteful sea. I kept the yacht under a press, according to orders, and the driving of her close-hauled, every luff trembling and the foam to leeward as high as the rail, fairly smothered the vessel forward; whilst as to her movements, it was dreary and aching enough, I can tell you, the wind sweeping out of clouds of spray forward and splitting with

Walter Besant

shrieks upon the ropes, and the canvas soaking up the damp till every stretch might have been owned for the matter of color by a coalman. 'Twas 'bout ship often enough, Mr. Robinson being full of anxiety and impatience, and watching the compass for a shift of wind as if he was a cat and there was a mouse in the binnacle. I could have sworn the handsome party would have been beam-ended by the dance; it turned the stomachs of two of the crew, anyhow, and one of them said that if he had known the 'Evangeline' was to cross the bay, he'd have found another ship; yet the lady took no notice of the weather. She'd come up dressed in waterproofs, and her beautiful face shining with the big eyes in it out of a hood; and the more the sea troubled the schooner, the more the vessel labored and showed herself uneasy, the more the lady would look pleased, laughing out at times, with plenty of music in her voice, I allow, but with a something in it and in the gleaming stare she'd keep on the plunging and streaming bows, that made me calculate—don't know why, I'm sure—that lovely as she was and beautiful as she was shaped, there was no more heart inside of her than there's pearls in cockles.

"Well, we had two days of this, passing a good many vessels; both steam and sail, that were getting all they could out of what was baffling us; then there was a shift of wind; it fell light, everything turned dry, and we went along with all cloths showing, sailing about five knots—not more, and I don't think less. When the change of weather came Mr. Robinson looked more cheerful. Seemed happier, he did, and I overheard him say to the party as they stood looking over the starn at the wake that ran away in two white lines with a gull, or two circling within a stone's throw in waiting for whatever the cook had to heave overboard—I heard him say:

"Every mile'll make it more difficult; besides," says he, with a sweep of his hand, 'what a waste this is! Williams,' he sings out to me, 'how fur off's the horizon?'

"'Why,' I answered, 'from this height I should say a matter of six mile and a half.'"

'And how fur distant, Captain Williams,' says the lady, smiling sweetly, and pretty nigh confusing my brains by the beautiful look she gave me, 'would a vessel like ours be seen?'

"I took time to think, with a squint at our mastheads—for we carried long sticks—and said, 'Well, call it twelve mile, mum. It's impossible to speak to a nicety.'

"And what," I heard Mr. Robinson observe, as I turned away, 'is twelve miles in this here watery wilderness of leagues?'

And then she gave a laugh, as if some one had made her feel glad; and it was all like music and poetry, I can tell you, her laughing, and his softness, and the water smooth, and the yacht sailing along as if she enjoyed it, like a hard-worked vessel out for a holiday.

"Time passed till it come on four o'clock on the afternoon of that day. There was a redness in the western heavens that betokened more wind, though the sun still stood high. Meanwhile the breeze hung steady. There was the smoke of a steamer away on our starboard quarter, and there was nothing else in sight. I took no notice of it, for smoke's not uncommon nowadays on the ocean; but whatever the vessel might be, the glances I'd take at her now and again made me see she was driving through it properly; for three-quarters of an hour after we had sighted it, the smoke was abeam, and the funnel raised up, showing that her course was something to the eastward of ours. I pointed the glass at her, and made out a yellow chimney and pole-masts—hull still below the horizon.

"Either a yacht, sir, or a Government dispatch boat—something of that kind, sir," says I to Mr. Robinson, who was sitting near me with the lady.

"He jumped up and took a look, and whilst he was working away with the telescope, the breeze comes along right out of the red sky abeam where the steamer was, with twice its former strength, roughening the blue water into hollows, and bowing

Walter Besant

down the yacht till the slope of her deck was like a roof. The crew jumped about shortening canvas, and the yacht began to snore as she felt the wind. On a sudden, and as if the steamer had only just then spied us, she altered her course by three or four points, as one could see by the swift rising of her hull, till, whilst the sun was still hanging a middling height over the sea line, you could see the whole of the vessel—a long, low craft of about one hundred and fifty tons—sweeping through the seas like an arrow, the smoke streaming black and fat from her small, yellow funnel, and her hull sinking out of sight one moment and reappearing the next in a sort of jump of the whole foaming wash, as if, by Jove, her screw would thrust her clean out of the water.

"The lady looked at her with a sort of indifference; but Mr. Robinson was pale enough as he handed me the glass, and said, 'Williams, see if you know her.'

"I took a look at her, and answered, 'It's hard to tell those steamers till you see their names, sir; but if she's not the Violet, belonging to General Coldsteel (of course these are false names), she's uncommonly like her. But, law bless us! how they're driving her! Why, there'll be a bust up if they don't look out. They'll blow the boilers out of her!'"

'Indeed, I never before saw any vessel rush so. She'd shear clear through some of the larger seas, and you didn't need watch her long to make you reckon you'd seen the last of her. Then Mr. Robinson, talking like a man half in a rage, half in a fright, orders me to pack sail on the schooner; but it was already blowing a single-reef breeze, and I had no idea of losing our spars, and so I told him very firmly that the yacht had all she needed, and that more would only stop her by burying her: and I had my way. But we were foaming through it, too; we wanted no more pressure; the freshening wind had worked the schooner into a fair nine knots, and it was first-rate sailing too, considering the character of the sea and the weight of the breeze. 'Twas now certain beyond all question that the steamer meant to close us, though I thought she had a queer way of doing it, for sometimes she'd head right at us, and then put her helm down and keep on a course parallel with ours, forging well ahead and then shifting the helm for a fresh run at us. There was no anxiety that I could see in the lady's looks, but Mr. Robinson was quite mightily bothered and worried and pale enough to make me suppose that all this meant a pursuit, with a capture to follow; and it was certain that whatever intentions the steamer had, there was nothing in the night which was approaching to promise us a chance of sneaking clear, for the sky was pure as glass, and it wouldn't be long after sundown before the moon would be filling the air with a light like morning.

Well, sir, fathom by fathom the steamer had her way of us. She had drawn close enough to let Mr. Robinson make out the people abroad. As for me, I was at the helm; for there was something in the maneuvering of the steamer that made me suspicious, and I wasn't going to trust any man but myself at the tiller. We held on as we were; we couldn't improve the schooner's speed by bringing the wind anywhere else than where it was; and no good was to be done by cracking on, even though it had, come to our dragging what we couldn't carry; for the steamer's speed was a fair fourteen if it was a mile, and our yacht was not going to do that, you know, or anything like it. The moon had arisen, and the sea ran like heaving snow from the windward, and by this time the steamer was about half a mile ahead of us, about three points on the weather bow. She was as plain as if daylight lay on her. All the time the party and Mr. Robinson had kept the deck, she taking a view now and then of the steamer with an opera-glass.

"Suddenly I yelled out, 'Mr. Robinson, by all that's holy, sir, that vessel there means to run us down! Lads,' I shouted, 'tumble aft quick, and see the boats all ready for lowering!'

"The lady jumped up with a scream, and seized hold of Mr. Robinson's arm, who seeming to forget what he was about, shook her off, and fell to raving to me to see that the steamer didn't touch us. By thunder, sir, there was the cowardly brute slanting her flying length as though to cross our hawse, but clearly aiming to strike us right amidships. I shouted to the men to make ready and 'bout ship, and a minute after I shoved the tiller over, and the yacht rounded like a woman waltzing. But before we had gathered way the steamer was after us. The lady sent up scream after scream. Mr. Robinson stood motionless, seeing as plain as I that if the steamer meant to sink us there was no seamanship in this wide world that could stop her; and I saw the men throwing off their shoes and half stripping themselves, ready for what was to come.

"The steamer headed dead to strike our weather-beam; she rushed at us with the foam boiling over her bows; once more I chucked the schooner right up into the wind, and the steamer went past us like a rocket under our stern. I looked at her and sha'n't ever forget what I saw. There was a white-haired man, with white whiskers and bareheaded, roaring and raging at us in the grasp of three or four seamen. 'Twas like a death-struggle. A chap who looked as if he had just seized the wheel was grinding it hard over to get away from us; and so the steamer fled past, more like a nightmare than a reality, and in a few minutes was standing with full speed to the norrard, where, in less than a quarter of an hour, she faded slick out of sight.

"It was some time after I had left the 'Evangeline' and was at home before I got to know the meaning of this here wonderful adventure. The party, it turned out, was no less than the wife of the general as owned the 'Violet,' and she was running away with Mr. Robinson. May be our men had talked about our going to the Mediterranean, but anyhow the general who was in London at the time, got scent that his wife had bolted with Mr. Robinson in the 'Evangeline,' and in less than twenty-four hours he was after us in his steamer. He tracked us by speaking the vessels we passed; and the light airs and calms we had encountered easily allowed him to overhaul quickly. And it turned out that when he had fairly sighted us, he sent the man at the wheel forward, and took the helm himself. The crew dursn't express their wonder aloud, though they knew he was no hand at steering, not to mention the mad agitation he was in, and they let him have his way when he headed the steamer for us, expecting that he merely wished to close us in order to speak; but when I put my helm down and the steamer passed, and they spied the general rounding his craft evidently to run us down, they threw themselves upon him to save their own lives as well as ours. That was the sight I saw as the steamer rushed past. A few moments after they had gone clear the poor old fellow was seized with an attack of apoplexy, which killed him right off, and thereupon they headed right away to England with the dead body aboard.

"What do you think of this for a yarn? Would any one suppose such vengefulness could exist in a white-haired man that had known his seventieth birthday? What did he want to go and try and drown me and my mates for? *We* weren't running away with the female party. But the world's full of romantic capering, sir; and I tell you what it is—'tain't all fair sailing even in yachts, modest and pretty as the diversion is."

ABOUT THE AUTHOR

Sir Walter Besant (August 14, 1836 Portsmouth - June 9, 1901 London), was a novelist and historian from London. His sister-in-law was Annie Besant.

The son of a mechant, he was born at Portsmouth, and attended school at St Paul's, Southsea, Stockwell Grammar, London and King's College London. In 1855, he was admitted as a pensioner to Christ's College, Cambridge, where he graduated in 1859 as 18th wrangler. After a year as Mathematical Master at Rossall School and a year at Leamington College, he spent 6 years as professor of mathematics at the Royal College, Mauritius. A breakdown in health compelled him to resign, and he returned to England and settled in London in 1867. He took the duties of Secretary to the Palestine Exploration Fund, which he held 1868-85. In 1871, he was admitted to Lincoln's Inn

He published in 1868 Studies in French Poetry. Three years later he began his collaboration with James Rice. Among their joint productions are Ready-money Mortiboy (1872), and the Golden Butterfly (1876), both, especially the latter, very successful. This connection was brought to an end by the death of Rice in 1882. Thereafter B. continued to write voluminously at his own hand, his leading novels being All in a Garden Fair, Dorothy Forster (his own favourite), Children of Gibeon, and All Sorts and Conditions of Men. The two latter belonged to a series in which he endeavoured to arouse the public conscience to a sense of the sadness of life among the poorest classes in cities. In this crusade Besant had considerable success, the establishment of The People's Palace in the East of London being one result. In addition to his work in fiction B. wrote largely on the history and topography of London. His plans in this field were left unfinished: among his books on this subject is London in the 18th Century.

Other works among novels are *My Little Girl*, *With Harp and Crown*, *This Son of Vulcan*, *The Monks of Thelema*, *By Celia's Arbour*, and *The Chaplain of the Fleet*, all with Rice; and *The Ivory Gate*, *Beyond the Dreams of Avarice*, *The Master Craftsman*, *The Fourth Generation*, etc., alone. London under the Stuarts, London under the Tudors are historical.

Choose from Thousands of 1stWorldLibrary Classics By

A. M. Barnard
Ada Leverson
Adolphus William Ward
Aesop
Agatha Christie
Alexander Aaronsohn
Alexander Kielland
Alexandre Dumas
Alfred Gatty
Alfred Ollivant
Alice Duer Miller
Alice Turner Curtis
Alice Dunbar
Allen Chapman
Alleyne Ireland
Ambrose Bierce
Amelia E. Barr
Amory H. Bradford
Andrew Lang
Andrew McFarland Davis
Andy Adams
Angela Brazil
Anna Alice Chapin
Anna Sewell
Annie Besant
Annie Hamilton Donnell
Annie Payson Call
Annie Roe Carr
Annonaymous
Anton Chekhov
Archibald Lee Fletcher
Arnold Bennett
Arthur C. Benson
Arthur Conan Doyle
Arthur M. Winfield
Arthur Ransome
Arthur Schnitzler
Arthur Train
Atticus
B.H. Baden-Powell
B. M. Bower
B. C. Chatterjee
Baroness Emmuska Orczy
Baroness Orczy
Basil King
Bayard Taylor
Ben Macomber
Bertha Muzzy Bower
Bjornstjerne Bjornson

Booth Tarkington
Boyd Cable
Bram Stoker
C. Collodi
C. E. Orr
C. M. Ingleby
Carolyn Wells
Catherine Parr Traill
Charles A. Eastman
Charles Amory Beach
Charles Dickens
Charles Dudley Warner
Charles Farrar Browne
Charles Ives
Charles Kingsley
Charles Klein
Charles Hanson Towne
Charles Lathrop Pack
Charles Romyn Dake
Charles Whibley
Charles Willing Beale
Charlotte M. Braeme
Charlotte M. Yonge
Charlotte Perkins Stetson
Clair W. Hayes
Clarence Day Jr.
Clarence E. Mulford
Clemence Housman
Confucius
Coningsby Dawson
Cornelis DeWitt Wilcox
Cyril Burleigh
D. H. Lawrence
Daniel Defoe
David Garnett
Dinah Craik
Don Carlos Janes
Donald Keyhoe
Dorothy Kilner
Dougan Clark
Douglas Fairbanks
E. Nesbit
E. P. Roe
E. Phillips Oppenheim
E. S. Brooks
Earl Barnes
Edgar Rice Burroughs
Edith Van Dyne
Edith Wharton

Edward Everett Hale
Edward J. O'Biren
Edward S. Ellis
Edwin L. Arnold
Eleanor Atkins
Eleanor Hallowell Abbott
Eliot Gregory
Elizabeth Gaskell
Elizabeth McCracken
Elizabeth Von Arnim
Ellem Key
Emerson Hough
Emilie F. Carlen
Emily Bronte
Emily Dickinson
Enid Bagnold
Enilor Macartney Lane
Erasmus W. Jones
Ernie Howard Pie
Ethel May Dell
Ethel Turner
Ethel Watts Mumford
Eugene Sue
Eugenie Foa
Eugene Wood
Eustace Hale Ball
Evelyn Everett-green
Everard Cotes
F. H. Cheley
F. J. Cross
F. Marion Crawford
Fannie E. Newberry
Federick Austin Ogg
Ferdinand Ossendowski
Fergus Hume
Florence A. Kilpatrick
Fremont B. Deering
Francis Bacon
Francis Darwin
Frances Hodgson Burnett
Frances Parkinson Keyes
Frank Gee Patchin
Frank Harris
Frank Jewett Mather
Frank L. Packard
Frank V. Webster
Frederic Stewart Isham
Frederick Trevor Hill
Frederick Winslow Taylor

Friedrich Kerst
Friedrich Nietzsche
Fyodor Dostoyevsky
G.A. Henty
G.K. Chesterton
Gabrielle E. Jackson
Garrett P. Serviss
Gaston Leroux
George A. Warren
George Ade
Geroge Bernard Shaw
George Cary Eggleston
George Durston
George Ebers
George Eliot
George Gissing
George MacDonald
George Meredith
George Orwell
George Sylvester Viereck
George Tucker
George W. Cable
George Wharton James
Gertrude Atherton
Gordon Casserly
Grace E. King
Grace Gallatin
Grace Greenwood
Grant Allen
Guillermo A. Sherwell
Gulielma Zollinger
Gustav Flaubert
H. A. Cody
H. B. Irving
H.C. Bailey
H. G. Wells
H. H. Munro
H. Irving Hancock
H. R. Naylor
H. Rider Haggard
H. W. C. Davis
Haldeman Julius
Hall Caine
Hamilton Wright Mabie
Hans Christian Andersen
Harold Avery
Harold McGrath
Harriet Beecher Stowe
Harry Castlemon
Harry Coghill
Harry Houidini

Hayden Carruth
Helent Hunt Jackson
Helen Nicolay
Hendrik Conscience
Hendy David Thoreau
Henri Barbusse
Henrik Ibsen
Henry Adams
Henry Ford
Henry Frost
Henry James
Henry Jones Ford
Henry Seton Merriman
Henry W Longfellow
Herbert A. Giles
Herbert Carter
Herbert N. Casson
Herman Hesse
Hildegard G. Frey
Homer
Honore De Balzac
Horace B. Day
Horace Walpole
Horatio Alger Jr.
Howard Pyle
Howard R. Garis
Hugh Lofting
Hugh Walpole
Humphry Ward
Ian Maclaren
Inez Haynes Gillmore
Irving Bacheller
Isabel Cecilia Williams
Isabel Hornibrook
Israel Abrahams
Ivan Turgenev
J.G.Austin
J. Henri Fabre
J. M. Barrie
J. M. Walsh
J. Macdonald Oxley
J. R. Miller
J. S. Fletcher
J. S. Knowles
J. Storer Clouston
J. W. Duffield
Jack London
Jacob Abbott
James Allen
James Andrews
James Baldwin

James Branch Cabell
James DeMille
James Joyce
James Lane Allen
James Lane Allen
James Oliver Curwood
James Oppenheim
James Otis
James R. Driscoll
Jane Abbott
Jane Austen
Jane L. Stewart
Janet Aldridge
Jens Peter Jacobsen
Jerome K. Jerome
Jessie Graham Flower
John Buchan
John Burroughs
John Cournos
John F. Kennedy
John Gay
John Glasworthy
John Habberton
John Joy Bell
John Kendrick Bangs
John Milton
John Philip Sousa
John Taintor Foote
Jonas Lauritz Idemil Lie
Jonathan Swift
Joseph A. Altsheler
Joseph Carey
Joseph Conrad
Joseph E. Badger Jr
Joseph Hergesheimer
Joseph Jacobs
Jules Vernes
Julian Hawthrone
Julie A Lippmann
Justin Huntly McCarthy
Kakuzo Okakura
Karle Wilson Baker
Kate Chopin
Kenneth Grahame
Kenneth McGaffey
Kate Langley Bosher
Kate Langley Bosher
Katherine Cecil Thurston
Katherine Stokes
L. A. Abbot
L. T. Meade

L. Frank Baum
Latta Griswold
Laura Dent Crane
Laura Lee Hope
Laurence Housman
Lawrence Beasley
Leo Tolstoy
Leonid Andreyev
Lewis Carroll
Lewis Sperry Chafer
Lilian Bell
Lloyd Osbourne
Louis Hughes
Louis Joseph Vance
Louis Tracy
Louisa May Alcott
Lucy Fitch Perkins
Lucy Maud Montgomery
Luther Benson
Lydia Miller Middleton
Lyndon Orr
M. Corvus
M. H. Adams
Margaret E. Sangster
Margret Howth
Margaret Vandercook
Margaret W. Hungerford
Margret Penrose
Maria Edgeworth
Maria Thompson Daviess
Mariano Azuela
Marion Polk Angellotti
Mark Overton
Mark Twain
Mary Austin
Mary Catherine Crowley
Mary Cole
Mary Hastings Bradley
Mary Roberts Rinehart
Mary Rowlandson
M. Wollstonecraft Shelley
Maud Lindsay
Max Beerbohm
Myra Kelly
Nathaniel Hawthrone
Nicolo Machiavelli
O. F. Walton
Oscar Wilde
Owen Johnson
P.G. Wodehouse
Paul and Mabel Thorne

Paul G. Tomlinson
Paul Severing
Percy Brebner
Percy Keese Fitzhugh
Peter B. Kyne
Plato
Quincy Allen
R. Derby Holmes
R. L. Stevenson
R. S. Ball
Rabindranath Tagore
Rahul Alvares
Ralph Bonehill
Ralph Henry Barbour
Ralph Victor
Ralph Waldo Emmerson
Rene Descartes
Ray Cummings
Rex Beach
Rex E. Beach
Richard Harding Davis
Richard Jefferies
Richard Le Gallienne
Robert Barr
Robert Frost
Robert Gordon Anderson
Robert L. Drake
Robert Lansing
Robert Lynd
Robert Michael Ballantyne
Robert W. Chambers
Rosa Nouchette Carey
Rudyard Kipling
Saint Augustine
Samuel B. Allison
Samuel Hopkins Adams
Sarah Bernhardt
Sarah C. Hallowell
Selma Lagerlof
Sherwood Anderson
Sigmund Freud
Standish O'Grady
Stanley Weyman
Stella Benson
Stella M. Francis
Stephen Crane
Stewart Edward White
Stijn Streuvels
Swami Abhedananda
Swami Parmananda
T. S. Ackland

T. S. Arthur
The Princess Der Ling
Thomas A. Janvier
Thomas A Kempis
Thomas Anderton
Thomas Bailey Aldrich
Thomas Bulfinch
Thomas De Quincey
Thomas Dixon
Thomas H. Huxley
Thomas Hardy
Thomas More
Thornton W. Burgess
U. S. Grant
Upton Sinclair
Valentine Williams
Various Authors
Vaughan Kester
Victor Appleton
Victor G. Durham
Victoria Cross
Virginia Woolf
Wadsworth Camp
Walter Camp
Walter Scott
Washington Irving
Wilbur Lawton
Wilkie Collins
Willa Cather
Willard F. Baker
William Dean Howells
William le Queux
W. Makepeace Thackeray
William W. Walter
William Shakespeare
Winston Churchill
Yei Theodora Ozaki
Yogi Ramacharaka
Young E. Allison
Zane Grey